The things you left: stories

Raki Kopernik

The things you left: stories

Raki Kopernik

for beaz, leona and monkey

Contents

There is more water than land on Earth.
There is more skin than muscle, more memory not used than
used, more dirty than clean places.

Sometimes I am so afraid of the ocean.

Homely

Behind the picture window on Twelfth and Grand, the one you can see from the street if you walk on the south side of the sidewalk and look up to the second floor, lives a ten-pound longhaired calico that spends her days looking out at the passing cars. Her eyes generally rest in coin slot-like slits and her limbs tuck under her body, like a chicken keeping her eggs warm. She doesn't jump when pots crash or dishes break against the plaster behind her because she has grown accustomed to these sounds.

Bertha and Tilda love the calico.

On a given day, if you look up to the second story, you might see the calico in her meditative state, the glass of the picture window vibrating from her purrs. You might also see shards of porcelain exploding like fireworks around her. Bertha and Tilda go to the thrift store down the street each week to buy new dishes. They are particularly fond of thin white Corningware, which breaks easily. Their therapist encourages Frisbee plate throwing.

You need to release your aggression, he says.

If the calico could speak English she would say, Your therapist needs therapy.

Bertha and Tilda throw the plates at each other as though they were, in fact, playing a game of Frisbee. But they don't try to catch. They are working with ducking and stepping out of the way. Neither of them played Frisbee as children, so occasionally their faces are marred with deep greens and purples. They have an extensive make-up collection.

In their plate tossing games, they also incorporate language.

Bertha likes to say things like, Why don't you turn your heart back on?

Tilda says, I'm fucked up, and, you expect too much.

Tilda works in a bookstore across town. She reads intellectual books by dead Russian novelists and connects deeply with the alcohol-soaked men who come into the bookstore off the street to use the bathroom. She wears argyle sweater vests to work, which Bertha thinks are nerdy and sweet.

I'm so homely, Tilda says.

Only when you wear sweater vests, Bertha says.

Bertha is a junior high school teacher, her excuse for sometimes acting like she's in junior high.

We are mirrors of our environment, she says.

Bertha and Tilda have lived on the second floor with the calico for two and a half years. Before she met Tilda, Bertha was happier. She was contentedly sleeping around, enjoying her junior high bachelor lifestyle.

Tilda has never been happy, although in the beginning of their relationship, she once said she felt peaceful.

Last week, in a particularly heated Frisbee toss, Tilda lost her left front tooth. Bertha was not happy with her achievement, but something inside of her throat released. She cried and threw up on the living room floor, then took Tilda to the emergency dentist. Tilda didn't cry. She opted not to have a new tooth put in, but rather, to leave the space open.

Do you think you're homely now? Bertha asked her.

Always on the inside, she said.

They know each other

It turns out they know each other. The one who broke my heart and the one who mended it. From their youth in Corvallis. White girls. Troublemakers.

We saw her, the one who broke my heart, at the café. I told her, the one who mended my heart, the story. How she broke it, my heart, because I loved her too much. Now I love the one who fixed my heart more.

She, the one I love more, told me how they ran together when they were nineteen. How she, the one who broke my heart, was awkward and a piano virtuoso. She still is.

She told me how they loved each other's girlfriends and then each other. You can do that when you're gay, love all your friends and their girlfriends and switch around like that. Sometimes.

At the café, the one I love now was eating rice and beans on corn tortillas. I was eating a Swiss Rueben on rye. I always get rye. The one I love more said I like rye because I'm Jewish. We do that, make inappropriate jokes. To show our love and that we can laugh at ourselves. I couldn't do that with the one who broke my heart. She would get defensive.

I didn't see what she was eating, the one who broke my heart, because my heart was beating too fast to look. My hands were shaking. We said hello and smiled and then, see you later. Then we got seated behind them, the heartbreaker and her music friend and their pit bull mutts. Outside on wooden benches, like the ones in parks for picnics. Because it turned out to be a nice day even though it had rained the night before.

When they left, she told me about their past, about how she, the one I love now, left her, the one who broke my heart, to move to Portland.

The one I love now broke the heart of the one who broke my heart. That made me feel good and then shallow and then good again.

Also because the one who broke my heart looked like she just woke up and her dirty sweatpants were pulled up to the knees. Scabs on her shins. Her dirty blonde hair, dirty from dirt not color. Like she'd just rolled around in a sandbox. Like a little kid. Not like the one I love now, whose shoes are always shined, and whose shirts are neatly pressed.

The red-lipped fedora girl

I met a girl with a fedora and a huge red mouth. She smiled all the time, a big wide smile. Her mouth was so big that when she opened it, I could see all the way down her throat to her heart. More than once, I almost fell into her mouth and down, into her body.

The fedora was dark gray with a light gray band and it lived, permanently, fixed on her head. She would flip upside down and still, the fedora stayed put. When she showered she put a plastic cap over it so it wouldn't get wet.

Every day, I visited her at the teahouse down the street where she worked. On warm days I drank bubble tea with aloe bubbles, and when it was cold, spicy chai with whole milk. At night we'd go to the bar down the street and play ping-pong, a soda on her corner of the table, a cheap beer on mine. Once in a while she had whiskey in her soda and even then, even with whiskey, her fedora stayed in place.

Our ping-pong game advanced to where the ball looked like a shooting star. People started to gather around us and cheer. Then the local news came. We got on TV and in the newspaper.

Red-lipped fedora girl and small hesher take ping-pong to outer space!

When she read that headline, she hugged me and kissed my forehead, leaving a big red lipstick mark from my right temple to my left. Then she looked in my eyes and I put my mouth on hers. She didn't swallow me, even though I thought she might. She just kissed my lips slowly and licked my gums. Her mouth tasted like a campfire. I licked her gums back. When we pulled our mouths apart, her lips were still perfectly red and her fedora sat in place, unmoved. I tried to ask her how it was possible but she put her fingertips on my mouth and said, let's drink coconut chai.

Okay, I said.

On her birthday I bought her a shiny black top hat, thinking she might want a change. She smiled in her Guy-Smiley way and kissed my cheek, leaving a red lipstick mark from my right ear to the edge of my mouth.

I'll put it on top of the Christmas tree, she said.

But you don't have a Christmas tree.

I'll get one for the hat, she said.

It was July. And she was Jewish. But she was good with plants.

For Rosh Hashanah, we ate apples with honey for a sweet new year.

This year I will change my style, she said.

I hoped that she would get a new hairdo and want to show it off. Instead she started wearing black thigh-high boots. Nothing to complain about, but I couldn't stop thinking about what was under the fedora.

By winter she had left wide red lipstick marks in various places on my body, like my arms, shoulder to elbow, and my lower back, hip-to-hip. Once, she kissed my butt and was able to cover both cheeks in one kiss.

When it finally snowed, she invited me to sleep under her down comforter to stay warm. We ate toast in her bed. She put my whole hand in her mouth, and it came out red with lipstick. I kissed her neck. Then we slept. She tossed and turned and still, the fedora stayed fixed in place.

In the morning I woke before her. Her lips were perfectly red, parted a little. I wanted her mouth to be opened wider so I could crawl inside and be warmed by her breath. But more than that, I wanted to take off the fedora. I touched its velvety rim between my thumb and fingers. I stroked the light gray band with the back of my hand. I put my wrist in the valley on top of the hat. She didn't wake. I stared. I watched her sleep. I touched her red mouth. I thought some more. How could I really know someone without ever seeing her cowlick?

I held the brim of the hat between the fingers of my right hand. I tugged upward as gently as I could. The hat didn't move. I tugged again, a little harder this time, and heard a faint tear. Nothing dramatic. I pulled a little more. Another undramatic tear. I kept going. Gentle tug. Little tear. Small pull. Rip rip. I kept pulling. Slowly. The hat lifted inch by inch. She slept through the whole the thing. When the hat was almost disengaged with her head, when her skin had undone itself, a small light shined from her forehead and then from the top of her head. I rested the fedora, still connected to the back of her head, on the pillow. My face was lit from the bright white light shining out of her head. She was a heat lamp, a spotlight, a lantern. I felt my pupils turn to slits. The light was blinding. I couldn't see anything else inside. I crawled in. It was warm and cramped but comfortable enough. I reached up and pulled the fedora shut, closed my eyes, and went back to sleep.

The broken piano

When I woke up the next morning and looked out the window, I saw that a piano had been dropped on my 1980 Oldsmobile, which was okay because the car was old and worth next to nothing. But after rubbing the sleep from my eyes and focusing, I noticed a pair of thin legs stretching like sandwich meat from between the roof of the car and the base of the piano, and a red high heel shoe swimming in a puddle of blood on the curb beside the whole mess. A small poodle was licking the shoe.

Five minutes later, the blonde walked by. A few seconds after that, a man. The man seemed to be following the blonde, but the blonde didn't know she was being followed. Neither of them noticed the piano on my car. Or the blood. The blonde said hello to the poodle, not the way people normally talk to animals, in a baby voice, but more like the way people say hello to someone they've just met formally, not really caring if they see the person again.

Hello dog, she said in her baritone voice, then kept walking.

I thought about yelling down to her because I thought I should do something about her being followed. I wasn't sure if she would remember me. A lot of time had passed since we last saw each other. Maybe five years. But her hair was the same. Same shade of yellow, same short messy cut. It seemed she still cut her own hair with those old blunt scissors she used to cut her toenails.

I wondered where she was going. I didn't know she was on the west coast. When she left, New York was the last place she said she could see herself. That she would never leave. At least not until she got famous.

When she loved me she hardly called me, so I didn't expect that she would find me after all this time, after not loving me for so long. But seeing her from the window, the top of her head and the sound of her scratchy voice, I wished she would call.

The piano on my car was dark brown wood and cracked down the middle, which probably happened from the impact of the fall. It looked like it might've been a nice piano before it was dropped. She would've liked it. She always wanted a piano but her big keyboard sounded just as good. I played piano too, but never in front of her because she was much better than I ever was.

Then I heard the sirens. The street cleared out and two fire trucks, an ambulance, and five cop cars surrounded my crushed car with the lady legs and the piano. The blonde turned to look. When she looked, the man ran away. Her eyes followed him and then landed on the piano.

Oh how sad, she said.

Fortune on the fridge

In September, as the summer began to wane and the air pulled cool moisture from the lakes, Layla went to Chang's Magic Dragon Breath to celebrate the first moments of autumn, her favorite season. She ordered a meal of Moo Shu vegetables with extra plum sauce. She watched as the server spread a dollop of sauce on each pancake with a spoon, then drop a small load of filling on top and roll it all up with chopsticks. She ate with her eyes closed, feeling each bite around her tongue, each sweet and tangy whiff through her nostrils, each slow swallow. When the fortune cookie came with the bill, she pulled apart its plastic wrapper and cracked it open. Before reading the fortune, she took a bite of the sweet almond cookie, closed her eyes again and savored the sticky flavor. Layla thought this experience might help her cheeks perk and bring on some joy. But it didn't. She retained a sadness in her body that she did not understand. Once swallowed, she opened her eyes and unfolded the paper: *If you're feeling down, try throwing yourself into your work.* She re-read the paper three times, folded it in half, stuffed it into her pocket, and went home. She would wait to eat the whole cookie until she understood its words fully.

When she got home, Layla placed the fortune on her fridge with a small Xena Warrior Princess magnet and went to sleep. She dreamed she found a dragon that breathed fire to warm her house but got overzealous and burned her house down. In the morning, she woke in a sweat. She got out of bed and went to look at the fortune on the fridge. She read it out loud: *If you're feeling down, try throwing yourself off a bridge.* She rubbed her eyes and read again: *If you're feeling down, try throwing a tantrum.*

Layla was not startled. She believed in the magic of fortune cookies. That day, she went to work as usual, in an office where she answered phones and had to wear beige pantyhose. During her lunch break, she ate her leftover Moo Shu and thought about her fortune. She wondered what it would tell her when she got home.

The sun was warm in the air that day and Layla decided to walk home instead of riding the bus. She walked across the tallest bridge in town, the one that separated the city into two parts, east and west. In the middle of the bridge, she stopped and looked down. She spat. It took a long time for the spit to reach the river below. She listened hard for the sound of her saliva landing in the water, but it was too far away. She didn't even see the tiny splash or the rings it probably made when it hit the river. She wondered how many people had stood where she was standing and what kinds of thoughts they had had. Did everyone spit off the bridge? It seemed like something everyone would do. She continued her walk, through the park and across from a schoolyard where she heard the shrill sounds of children playing and crying. She felt glad she was no longer a child, remembering how hard it was to be so small and not be able to communicate.

The first thing she did when she got home was look at the fortune on the fridge: *If you're feeling down, try throwing knives.* She read it out loud and then said to the fridge: If you're feeling down, try throwing pottery. If you're feeling down, try throwing pottery against the wall. If you're feeling down, try throwing a party.

She made a to-do list:
1.read a book about knife throwing
2.take a pottery class
3.throw a plate against the wall and see how that feels.
4.have a party for people you like

Over the next two months, as fall faded into winter and the rain turned to snow, she practiced throwing her cheap, thrift store knives at a corkboard next to the fridge. She developed a pretty good spin. She took a ceramics class at the community center every Monday evening, making as many plates, bowls, mugs, and disfigured containers as she could pump out. At the end of the class, she brought all her dishes home and threw them, one by one, against the wall. Indeed, this felt good. She invited all the people she loved to her apartment for a party. She served Red Hots candies and jalapeño poppers on the one plate she saved from the ceramics class that didn't break, even though she threw it. At the end of the party, everyone went up to the roof of the building with a boom box and danced on the snow to *Oh what a feeling when you're dancing on the ceiling.*

Layla looked around at her friends. She took a deep breath, watching her exhale escape in a cold, white cloud.

The girl I never knew

From behind and little to the right, there's no neck, just a long triangle of yellow hair. Escaped strands move around in the wind of the AC. A shoulder splits the yellow triangle on the side, so some of the hair falls forward, especially when she looks down to make a doodle in her notebook. The shoulder is covered in a red synthetic fabric with two shades of purple and turquoise flowers. The fabric looks like it doesn't breathe, and like a dress a five year old would wear.

The pattern on the dress continues down her back and likely down her thighs and knees. You can't see her face, but if you look between the legs of the chair, there is a foot encased in black fishnet with a brown leather slipper-like shoe dangling from the toes. If you lean forward, you might catch a glimpse of a profile. In profile, her upper lip extends a little farther over her bottom lip, like the Simpsons characters, but not so dramatic. She is cute, and in a few years the cute will turn to beautiful.

We are at a lecture about writing. I can tell she's not listening because she keeps making doodles in her notebook, and I am not listening because I am watching her doodling over her shoulder. The lecture does not matter and will not matter. What matters is that I notice her and, in this moment, she doesn't notice me notice. In two weeks there will be a party. She will be drinking a bright pink alcoholic drink and I will be drinking gin and I will tell her I have noticed her, and she will pretend she hasn't noticed me, but I will know that she has. We have been in a class together, we have smiled at each other, she has seen me watch her doodle.

At the party, we will have a drunk conversation and she will flirt with me and I will flirt back, knowing nothing will happen. She's not too young but I feel like she is too young for me. She's in a different place in her life, a place I was in so long ago that seeing her is nostalgic and uncomfortable. After the drunk party conversation, her friends will drag her away and I will go to sleep. The next day, I will watch her doodle at another lecture, and she will look up and see me. She'll smile and I'll smile and then she'll go back to her doodle and I will try to listen to the lecture.

I go to parties with my cat

We ended up in Randomville, Arizona. Sami and I go there often, but I don't know the place well. In Arizona you can sit outside without feeling air on your skin. We sat at an outdoor cafe eating onion bagels and cucumbers when a girl that looked like a girl I went to high school with came over to our table and invited us to a house party. Sami was on the prowl, so right away she said, yes.

Okay let's go, the girl said.

We followed the girl for a few blocks and arrived at the party. I knocked on the door, even though I didn't know whose house we were at, and an extremely tall person answered. The door answerer noticed my noticing her tallness and said, Oh I'm just wearing stilts for a second because, you know, I just am. Then she said her name, which was the same as mine.

I said, Sami she has the same name as me.

The person said, I don't go by *she*.

I said, oh sorry I mean *they*.

Then they said, no I go by *he*.

He was deeply offended so I thought I got off to a bad start at a party where I knew no one. Sami was already gone, flirting shamelessly with girls. I walked away, alone.

As is often the case in Arizona, there were cats all over the party. My cat included. In the bathroom line, I told someone that my cat came to the party and she gave me a look like, who do you even know here that you think you can bring your cat. So I quickly reassured her that my cat doesn't fight with other cats and is very nice to people. She was gone before I finished my explanation. Maybe she didn't really have to go to the bathroom. Most of the people at the party seemed to be in their own dense bubbles and I didn't know the secret password. So I walked room to room around the party, giving Sami time to flirt and possibly make out with someone, and to check out the cats. I kept reaching toward cats I thought were my cat, only to see a foreign marking, like a white spot on the tail. I started to wonder if I was still a good cat mom if I couldn't recognize my own cat of eleven years in a sea of other cats I'd never known.

I called out my cat's name and she came running to me without a meow. I picked her up and told her it was time to go home, even though I wasn't sure how we would get there. I wasn't as distressed as Dorothy trying to get to back to Kansas, but I closed my eyes anyway and tried her trick, *there's no place like home there's no place like home there's no place like home.*

There's no such thing as still

The squareness of the lower part of her face was jarring when her shoulders were exposed. She didn't live in her shoulders or in that part of her face. She lived from the eyes up. The rest was a cartoon, a picture that seemed to belong to someone else. She was a little ugly, even to those who loved her. Love is a slipping clutch. That's what happens when it starts to go. A thousand dollars and the engine revs high, but the body doesn't move forward. Like the car doesn't live together with its engine. A metal carcass with hollow parts.

It's not that she was hollow. She was just full of holes, looking away while everyone's fire filled her with fissures. Bull's eye to the sternum every time.

Her curtains were brown, and her bed was a single. She never took off her underwear but you did and that was okay with her. She might've liked it, your nudity. It was hard to tell what she liked about you. Her eyes stared, which sometimes felt like love and sometimes like the way kids stare at you on the bus, confused and intrigued. Sometimes the staring was empty.

This is what pulled you in in the first place. Eye contact melts your bones.

The thing is, even when you're waiting, you're still thinking, knitting, cracking your knuckles. There's no such thing as still. Hold your breath and nothing stops. It took you too long to know that she would never let out her breath in your face. She would just stare, quiet, turning blue. Inside your chest the oyster was cracked, and a pre-teen pearl was growing.

The clutch controls power and motion. The brake stops everything. Both prevent something and both make something happen.

Next to the single bed was an orange lamp, too big for the small room. And next to that a wood paneled desk, also too big. Too big like the squareness of her jaw and the space you made for her. Her mouth was also big, but not too big. Just full. Perfect to kiss in the morning. There was nothing ugly about her mouth. You'd like to have her mouth alone and the feeling of it kissing you back, the way she let go in the moment of a kiss without eyes or thoughts.

I want to cut your hair

It hangs dark, thick, smooth halfway between your eyelids. If you don't push it to the side, you can't see. Or you see like looking through a black mourning veil. From the front it's shaggy. From the side a three-inch ponytail that holds the back half of your head, sliced like in anatomy book figures, right left slice, top bottom slice, front back slice. The ponytail starts at the slice.

I need a haircut, you say. Your hair is a permanent hat. When you want me to hear you, you slide the front with your fingertips to the side, hard, so the roundness of your brown eyes is undeniable. And your forehead becomes real. When you don't want to know, you do a mild shake looking down, so the front falls heavy and your eyes are just bottom lashes.

I'm coming to your two-room apartment above the Rose Café with sharp scissors used only for cutting hair. Nothing else. The stairs are wide enough for two extravagant renaissance ball gowns to fit side by side. I feel small. The stairs are dirty, pissed on, discolored and abused. I would not bring a ball gown anywhere near them. I walk up. I like the way my boots sound against their grime. Your door is the first one on the left at the top. You leave it a crack open, so I know you're in there. I smell your cologne in the hallway. I don't like perfume, but you are different than what I like. I inhale deep subtle jasmine and the way my dad smells after he shaves. Aqua Velva. I hear you change the record from unfamiliar electronic reggae to Fleetwood Mac, Rumors. I stand outside your door smelling you, listening to you, imagining you and your hair moving around the little space. I wait. I don't knock. I don't do anything. If you weren't expecting a haircut, I might stand there all day.

I push open the door. It creaks a little. You're facing the window away from the door. You don't hear me come in. I stand in the doorway and watch you dance, singing with Stevie Nicks. When you turn around and see me you don't flinch. You keep smiling singing dancing. You dance over to me and I drop my bag. We harmonize with Stevie. When the song ends, you turn the volume down and pull a chair into the middle of the kitchen. The heat is turned up high and your apartment is hot the way it always is. My house is drafty. Your New York-in-the-fifties apartment with the uneven wood floors and shared shitty bathroom in the hall. I wonder who cleans the bathroom. Looks like no one.

I take off my coat hat scarf sweatshirt. It's always T-shirt weather at your place. You sit in the plastic chair and take off your shirt. I've never seen the skin of your chest or back. I'm surprised by your lacey black bra. It's girlier than I imagined you'd wear. I want to touch it, but I don't. You don't seem to notice me swallow.

Here's what I want, you say. You do a sweep around the bangs with your right hand and a cutting motion in the back with your left hand. Two inches. I move in a circle around you, touching your hair, pulling it lightly out and down. I run my fingers through your scalp to soften your hair and relax you. You close your eyes. I tug on your earlobes. Your skin feels like a velvet painting. I pull my scissors out of their protective case and run the blades against my shirt even though they are already clean. You wait, still and patient in the plastic chair. I put my right thumb into one hole of the scissors and my right middle finger into the other hole. I snap the scissors a few times. They feel like butter. Always. With my left hand I comb the back of your hair. The ponytail part. I let some of it fall from my fingers but keep hold of a small chunk. I take the scissors to your hair and I begin.

I almost never cut straight across. I position the scissors vertically, blades pointing down, and I start to slice. One small section at a time. Thick black pieces gather around your neck and shoulders. I wipe them away from time to time. Occasionally I blow them off and they float through the air around your body in slow motion. Sometimes I turn the scissors vertical the other way, tips pointing up, to blend the sides. I do the same in the front.

Close your eyes, I tell you. Then I take the scissors at an angle between vertical and horizontal to slice across, keeping with the angle of your bangs, taking them a little shorter, bit-by-bit. I blow the hairs off your face. This may be one of the only times it's okay to nonconsensually blow in someone's face. You shake your head to help the hairs fall. Your hair settles. I run my fingers through it messing it up.

Shake your head again, I say. You touch your hair.
Feels good, you say.
Looks good, I say.

You can't shake the front over your eyes anymore. I walk around to the back to double check my work. I comb the back with my fingers again then wipe your shoulders with my palms. I blow on your neck. I want to touch the front of your clavicles. I don't. But my hands rest on your shoulders a little bit longer.

Weeds are more independent

The first thing I noticed was gray smoke coming out of the dryer vent. The second thing, a tiny flame. I didn't want my parent's house to burn down, the house I grew up in, the house that smells like being small and clean laundry the way only my mom can make laundry smell. I didn't want the house to burn, and certainly not because of my dirty scumbag clothes struggling to get clean.

I was out in the neighbor's yard, in the little garden Emma used to plant every summer when she still lived there, now overgrown with weeds but still beautiful. The weeds make yellow and purple flowers. Who decides what makes something a weed anyway? Weeds are more independent than domesticated plants. They don't need people. I was there in the yard I always admired as a kid but never went into because it was Emma's special garden. She was nice, but I wasn't invited over. I saw the gray smoke get darker and the flame grow big and small and big again. I ran over, into the house, down the stairs to the basement toward where I thought the dryer was, the one from the seventies with that crank nob like the nob on our black and white TV. The basement was bigger than I had remembered. It was a dark maze made up of dozens of rooms with single, swinging light bulbs that cast shadows around the concrete walls and floors.

I was scared. This basement that I've known for almost four decades. It wasn't the first time I felt scared down there. But this time, I was scared in a different way. The lighting and the vastness of the space, the smoke, which began to fill my lungs, the fire I needed to extinguish, and the clothes I needed to rescue.

I looked up and found the shiny silver of the dryer vent strapped between boards in the ceiling. That would be my breadcrumb trail. I followed the vent through room after room until the panic of the fire began to fade. There were no fire sirens, no water, and, as far as I knew, nothing had changed outside.

I found the dryer. It was like an old friend. And it was no longer aflame. I scooped my clothes out into a plastic laundry bin and left them there at the base of dryer to deal with later. I took a deep breath and walked toward what looked like a natural light. The darkness of the basement opened into a small dance studio surrounded by windows, half above ground with wood floors and mirrors on the walls.

I did a pirouette and a grande jeté leap, walked up the stairs into the open air, and back into the weed the garden to pick some yellow and purple flowers for a bouquet.

The lady is a cat

The clock blinked 12:00, 12:00, 12:00, the way it does when the power has gone out. Her comforter felt warm from the sun filtering through the dirty window glass. But the air was bitter cold. She sighed a white puff of breath and rolled her thin frame to the side of the bed, up and out towards the bathroom, that one loose floor tile shifting under her weight with a clink.

The cat jumped off the bathroom counter and walked to his food dish, waiting for her to fill his dish with kibble after her morning crap. On her way out of the bathroom, she looked in the mirror. She stared into her own icy blue eyes, pressed her palm to the hardness of the mirror and didn't smile. Like repeating a word so many times until it sounds foreign, she looked at her eyes, minutes passing, until she didn't recognize herself.

The phone rang. The kettle whistled. She didn't remember lighting the stove. It was too early to answer the phone, although she was unsure of the time. She went to the kitchen and made a cup of black tea, with milk to soften the bitter edge. The milk turned the blackness a deep purple, like a day-old bruise. She looked into the cup the way she had looked into the mirror. It's color, it's heat and sweet smell pulled her in, and she wanted to be tiny, to crawl inside and sink to the cup's womb-like bottom.

Where are you? Her sister's voice. Are you there?

She drew her face closer to the tea.

I know you're there. Pick up the phone.

She walked to the answering machine and lifted the phone receiver.

I'm here, she said.

It's time, her sister said.

I'm not ready.

The funeral's in an hour. I'm coming over.

She put the phone back into its place and went to the bedroom to get dressed. First, she made the bed, shaking out the blankets. A cat whisker, perfectly straight and white, rested on the pillow. She picked it up, ran it through her thumb and forefinger. Its thick end poked into her palm, then she slid it between her teeth. The cat made a thump sound jumping in through the open window in the bathroom.

Pssst pssst kitty, she called.

The cat came in purring. He shook himself off and jumped on the bed, rubbing his head against her thigh.

Look what I found, she said to the cat.

He sniffed the whisker, then she ran her fingers through his attached whiskers and down his back to the end of his puffy black tail. She lay back, resting her head where she had found the whisker on the pillow. He climbed onto her belly, closed his eyes, and continued to purr. She felt the room darken, the way light changes when a cloud crosses the sun. With her right hand, she stroked the cat, whose body now felt heavier and fuller against her own body. When her hand touched his back, she found a woman's naked body.

She moved her hand slowly up and down the back and down around the butt. The skin was soft the way the cat's fur was, and her hand slid smooth and easy. She didn't feel scared or surprised, just noticed the weight and the shape, the texture and the pleasure of sensation. But soon her lungs began to compress from the weight. She tried to deepen her breath and to move the rest of her body, to push this body off of hers or wiggle away. She opened her eyes, felt her body move as she willed it to, but could also see that her body was still. Her body had no weight, as if it were not solid or real, and her breath seemed farther away each time she tried to take in air. The more she struggled, the more difficult it was to move, until finally she could not even move the parts she was previously able to move. She took one more deep breath with all the energy she had left and forced her eyes wider.

Her body jerked. There was a loud sound like the crash of a firework. The cat was lying on her chest, almost at her throat, purring, asleep. Sun still shone through the dirty window. She looked at her fingers, wiggled them, saw them and felt them move. Her sister was knocking at the door.

The favor

Listen, my mom said over the phone, I want you to know you have a favor owed to you. You know, *a favor.* All you have to do is let Uncle Louie know and he'll take care of it. Anything.

I imagined she winked when she said, *favor.*

My mother is a storyteller. I never know if she's making things up. I don't ask.

My mom makes lasagna and baked ziti and anything with red sauce, *gravy*, better than anyone but my nana and her nana. When she was a kid, my mom sat on the laps of thick cigar smoking men at mafia meetings. They gave her M & M's in a glass candy dish and she pretended to feed the red ones to her doll. She says she was too little to remember what they talked about, but we know they talked about things she can't repeat.

My mom always says, the world is full of assholes and the longer you live the more of them you'll know. If some of these assholes were no longer here, would that be so bad?

My mom says, the government is too corrupt to deal with such delicate matters as capital punishment. Innocent people get hurt when the government is involved. That's why you need an inside job, for certainty. Quick and painless no harm done.

The day my mom called and told me about *the favor*, I thought about the girl. She hadn't broken my heart and I had never loved her. She hadn't killed anyone. We had never been close. I thought about her for a different reason.

I met her as the girlfriend of an acquaintance. The acquaintance was a handsome man, a friend of a friend, who helped my friend build a deck on the back of his house. The acquaintance wore work boots and always had dirt on his rugged hands. I found the acquaintance nice to look at and friendly enough to drink beers with while he worked on the deck. We became friends but considered each another acquaintances. Outside of the deck-building project, we didn't spend time together, though we occasionally ran into each other at the bar or at the monthly square dance at the Vet's hall. I met her at one of the square dances.

I ended up dancing with him in one of the circles. We held hands, which was customary of that particular dance. We also smiled at each other, which was not customary but natural. She noticed that I liked looking at her boyfriend. I like looking at a lot of people. Some more than others, but most have something of interest. She said nothing to me that night.

I met her again a few days later in front of the bagel shop. I was talking to my friends about how much I appreciate a salt bagel with cream cheese and capers, when she came around the corner.

She said, stay away from my boyfriend you slut.

I said, I don't care about your boyfriend what are you talking about.

You heard me, she said, don't show your face around here or else.

One of my friends said, calm down don't start threatening people.

She said, I wasn't talking to you. Then she walked away fast and disappeared into the wind, like a ghost.

I ran into the acquaintance later that day at the bar and told him what happened. He laughed.

I met her again a week after the bagel shop incident at my front door. She knocked, I opened, she screamed.

If you don't stop talking to my boyfriend, I don't know what I'll do but I'm capable of a lot.

I said, hold on come in let's talk about this.

We have nothing to talk about, she said. She turned and left and again, disappeared fast as if she had never been there.

I don't know how she got my address. I started to feel nervous.

What I knew was that she was having an experience that had nothing to do with me. What I also knew was that I lived in a small town. There's no space in small towns.

The last time I met her was at the grocery store. Between the home visit and the store, I had seen him twice: once at the bar, again, and once at the hardware store buying washers for the kitchen sink. I told him about the home visit, and he laughed again.

You have to do something, I said.

She's crazy but harmless, he said.

At the grocery store I was buying olives for dirty martinis. I saw her at the end of the aisle, far enough away that I could turn and walk the other way, which is what I did. But we had a moment of eye contact. I knew she knew I was there. I pretended I hadn't seen her, hoping she might evaporate into the air like she had before. I went to the produce section and found her staring hard at me across the organic carrots. I walked the other way. I got some chips and she was there, laser eyes. I went to the canned goods, the juice, the frozen foods, the cold and sinus. She was everywhere. When I got to the ethnic foods she was close. I thought I smelled her body odor. I looked at her, into her spiral eyes, little flames glowing around her pupils, and smiled. Not a nice smile. A smile that said, you don't scare me I don't care about you. Even though I was scared. Even though I was no longer able to sleep with the fear of her breaking into my house and boiling my cat, Fatal Attraction style. Or standing over me in the dark of night with a chef's knife. She was a ghost, ethereal, everywhere.

I walked toward the checkout. I could see her in my periphery. I turned toward her and saw in her face that, this time, something else would happen, like when cats pull their ears back hard and you know they're about to bite you. Like a slingshot. Ready set go. I saw her pull back before she propelled forward. And then, she charged me. In less than two seconds I thought, you can step to the side, you can put out your fist and punch, or you can do nothing. There was no more time after that to decide. She ran toward me and spit a wad of saliva in my face. I stood, grocery basket in hand, saliva oozing down my face, still, like a block of cement. And then again, she was gone.

I wiped my face on the sleeve of my shirt and went through the checkout. The cashier asked me if I was okay. The other cashiers came up and asked if I was okay. The rest of the grocery store clerks came over and asked if I was okay.

Yes I'm okay I'm okay I'm fine.

When I got home, I put my groceries away and made a dirty martini with the new olives. I put on my sweatpants and washed my face and hands with hot water and lavender soap. I sat in my comfy chair, took a gulp of the martini, ate an olive, and picked up the phone. He answered after two rings.

Hey Uncle Louie, I said, you got a minute?

Tuna

Melvin Bootstring was a tuna loving man. He especially loved tuna out of a can. With salt and juice. Plain. The kind for making tuna salad sandwiches and tuna melts.

Melvin lived happily alone in a modest house built on a small hill. He stocked up on canned food for emergency, in case of an earthquake, and every three months he would rotate the food out, eating the goods then re-stocking. He bought canned goods from the Grocery Store Outlet because it was cheap. He called it the *gross-out* because most of the food in the store was old. And occasionally gross.

Recently, he bought a case of tuna cans for five dollars. There are one hundred cans of tuna in a case. The case sat in his basement with the rest of the emergency canned goods for the allotted three months. When it was time to eat the emergency goods, he made tuna casseroles with canned green beans and canned corn. He made tuna salad with mayonnaise, celery, pickles and onions, and canned black beans. He turned the salad into sandwiches. He made tuna melts with canned baked beans and Swiss cheese from the gross-out that wasn't gross. And he ate canned minestrone or split pea soup with tuna on the side. Once in a while, in moments of low blood sugar, he ate tuna straight out of the can. For three weeks Melvin ate tuna every day until all the other emergency canned goods were eaten and he was left with a stack of canned tuna. Then he began to restock the rest of the goods.

Three months later the rotation began again. He made soba noodles with tuna and ginger soy sauce. He made tuna-biscuit rolls and tuna jambalaya. He had tuna and rice with peas, tuna and quinoa with cashews and peanut sauce, tuna paella and tuna with turnips until, again, all the other emergency goods were gone, and he was left with a stack of tuna cans.

Melvin Bootstring did not get sick of eating tuna. He did, however, wonder how long a can of tuna would last. At what point would it make a person sick? Canned foods last. That's why he stocked up and why canned goods are emergency food. But he knew it was important to maintain the rotation, that nothing is good forever.

One day as he was restocking the basement on his third round since he bought the case, he picked up a can of tuna and looked at the date printed on its side. This can of tuna was said to be out of date a year and two months prior. That meant that when he bought the case it was already out of date. He had not gotten sick from eating it but in that moment, he decided it was no longer a healthy choice. He counted the cans of tuna. Fifty-three.

Melvin Bootstring was not a wasteful man. Fifty-three cans of out-of-date tuna were not trash. Nor, however, were they food.

For the next several days, Melvin thought about tuna three times a day. Each time he ate he tried to figure out what to do about the old cans. And because he'd gotten himself into this, he would not eat new tuna until he could figure out what to do with the tuna he already had.

Why don't you feed it to the cat, a friend suggested.

For a week Melvin gave the cat tuna once a day. After a few days the cat refused any other food and began following him around, whining and getting under Melvin's feet nearly causing him to fall down the stairs.

Why don't you donate it, the friend suggested.

Melvin mulled over the idea but decided that if he wouldn't eat the food for fear it was not healthy, he could not instigate someone else eating it and possibly getting sick.

The friend had no more ideas. Melvin began to decline. He would pass by sandwich shops and delis, pressing his nose to the glass cases, gawking at tuna salad sandwiches.

Fresh made today, the shop workers would say.

Want a taste? they'd ask.

I'll have the roasted veggie sandwich.

He would not cross his own boundary. Each day he thought about tuna and each day after returning home from deli temptation, he went into the basement and looked at the cans. Some days he'd pick up a can and decide it didn't matter, that he was just going to eat it. But two steps up from the basement he'd turn around and put the can back in the stack.

He began to dream about tuna. Little cans with fins swimming in the ocean around him. Multi-colored neon cans with wings, flying around his house. Tinny voices coming up from the basement, Melvin please, don't deny us. We need you.

For the first time in his life, Melvin Bootstring decided to go to therapy. He opened the phonebook to *therapists*, closed his eyes, and pointed to a name:

Dr. Fishcake, licensed to help you tighten your screws.
This seemed appropriate enough.

What is your problem? Dr. Fishcake asked at their first appointment.

I don't know what to do with all the tuna, Melvin said.

Throw it away and move on with your life, Dr. Fishcake said.

I'm not that kind of man.

What kind of man are you?

Not that kind.

When Melvin arrived for their second appointment the following week, Dr. Fishcake was eating a tuna salad sandwich.

Sorry. I'll be done in just a minute, the doctor said.

Melvin drooled a puddle around his feet.

You like tuna, Dr. Fishcake said.

How did you get that name?

It's Greek. It used to be Fishakakus. Would you like to tell me about the tuna?

If I believed in marriage, I would marry tuna in a can, Melvin said.

I understand why you can't throw it away.

Melvin had only one more appointment with Dr. Fishcake, in which the doctor said:

Shit or stand. You can't sit with your pants down for the rest of your life.

Melvin blinked.

When he got home, he blinked again. He took a breath. Another blink. He went down to the basement and collected cardboard boxes and crates. He took the boxes and crates into the house, lined them up in rows of five, and began to put his belongings inside of them: plates, bowls and mugs from the kitchen, shirts, slacks and socks from his dressers, novels, the dictionary, an encyclopedia collection off the shelves, floral print towels, a tube of cinnamon toothpaste and the toilet scrubber from the bathroom. Then he opened the phonebook to *movers*, closed his eyes, and pointed: *No Beef Movers.*

For the next week, Melvin bought the newspaper every day until he found a small, second story apartment with no basement on the other side of town. *No Beef* came the following week and took Melvin's boxes, his couch, a table and chairs, a desk, a futon, and three bookshelves to the new apartment.

For his first meal at his new home, Melvin baked a fresh, whole tuna in the oven with lemon and butter. He let the cat lick the plate when he finished eating. That night he dreamed he was flying, free and alone and happy.

The bones unhinge

One by one, her bottom teeth began to loosen and fall out. She poked her tongue around the softness of her gums, feeling the separation where each tooth began to unhinge. She tasted the metallic tang of blood, a familiar sensation from childhood. Back then, it was exciting to lose teeth. There was cool-kid status when someone lost a tooth, a step toward growing up. But now, as an adult, she didn't feel cool. She felt panic.

She tried not to hassle the teeth as they became loose, hoping they might fuse back into place, gums reabsorbing teeth roots. Sometimes, she thought, ignoring a problem makes it go away. She closed her eyes and thought of kittens. She thought of swimming in the ocean. She thought of eating key lime pie. But no amount of ignoring prevented her teeth from divorcing her gums. She began to feel the kind of panic you feel when cops show up at your door in the middle of the night, strobing red and blue lights, and you know someone you love is not okay. Or when you see a car about to hit you in slow motion, unable to stop what you know will happen. Stomach crashing panic.

She took a deep breath and tried to press the dread out of her mind. She looked at the teeth in her hands, turning them over one by one, admiring their pearl-like smoothness, their glossy eggshell color, their strength. She closed her eyes again and hoped an idea would come to her. How could she reconnect her teeth to her gums, realign them perfectly back up in her mouth?

The first tooth she examined was from the left side of her mouth, medium in size. It was that first wide tooth after the thin front teeth. Its roots hung down like silk rope, cream colored and healthy looking, as far as she could tell. She poked her tongue around the space the tooth left and enjoyed the sensation. It was the bottom row, which seemed better than the top. Although without the bottom row, the top would likely be useless. At the same moment, another tooth fell out. It was the same tooth she had been examining but on the other side. She tried to hold it in place with her tongue to prevent it from unhinging, but it wouldn't stay put. She reached into her mouth and took the tooth between her fingers and placed it into her palm. This tooth looked different from its twin on the other side. It was wrapped in a band of plastic and it looked plastic. She tried to remember all the dental work she'd had done in high school and junior high. The memories didn't come. But she felt positive about the tooth being synthetic. It meant she might be able to glue it back into place, as it had probably been glued once before.

She went to the bathroom mirror and smiled wide. Not a happy smile, a smile to examine. Her top row of teeth looked big, as usual. She began to pull back her bottom lip to inspect the spaces in the bottom row. She was nervous about what she would find, what her mouth would look like. She thought about how challenging it would be to eat without bottom teeth, though not too bad to smile. She thought about how she would change the way she engaged with people, that she would shift into a quiet, mysterious introvert, keeping her smiles to a grin and her words to a minimum. She thought she would probably no longer be able to whistle, a skill she was pretty good at. On the flip side, she thought she would save a lot of time and money not having to floss an entire row of teeth. Or maybe she would get a solid set of dentures and no one would ever know. Dentistry is quite advanced these days.

She was nervous to look, but she knew she had to.

She pinched her bottom lip with the thumb and first finger of each hand on each side and continued to pull the lip down. What she felt was not what she saw.

What she saw was a complete row of bottom teeth, all intact.

Pressure

It was an outpatient surgery, local anesthesia. When she arrived at the office, the nurse let her hold the implants. They were square and wrapped in white canvas cloth, but squishy underneath. She was surprised by their shape and look and wondered if it was a good idea that she hold them with her bare hands, seeing as they were about to be implanted inside of her body. She kept these thoughts to herself.

The nurse had her lie on her back on an operating table and injected the anesthetic into the side of her breast. A middle-aged TV-style doctor came in. She looked at his salt-and-pepper hair and then at his face. He smiled. She told him she was nervous about the pain.

You'll just feel a bit of pressure, he said.

Pressure was, in fact, what she already felt.

It's really no big deal, he said.

He made a quick cut across the top of her left breast and pulled the flesh up to make space for the implant. She took an uneasy breath. When he finished the left side, he sewed the top of her breast with one quick motion as if drawing a line with a pen, then did the same on the other side. The whole thing took three minutes.

When it was over, she walked around the doctor's office. Her breasts felt heavy and tender. She felt her nipples through her shirt. They were perkier and situated much higher on each breast.

Now you don't have to wear a bra, the doctor told her.

She remembered her sister-in-law letting her feel her implanted breasts in the back of the car on the way to the theater.

I never wear a bra, she had said.

She envied that part. But she wondered what people would say when they saw her the next day with her new, giant tits. She hadn't told anyone she was going to do this. In fact, she couldn't remember when or why she had made this decision in the first place. Perhaps society had gotten the best of her.

She asked the doctor if he could take them out. She worried her original breasts would be stretched out, but thought that would be better than fake, canvas ones. He told her she'd have to wait a month for the insertion points to heal before he could do anything. She'd have to walk around braless and buoyant for a month. She tried to think of something positive about the whole situation, but the worry that people would think she was crazy overpowered any thoughts of comfort or fun. She touched her new rack again. She gave a gentle squeeze, fearing they would pop. And the weight of them, though spry, pulled against her body.

She realized there was nothing she could do but wait. She had made her bed and now she had to lie, perky and braless, in its consequence.

She sat down in a plastic chair in the waiting room of the doctor's office and thought about what kinds of clothes would cover up the bad decision she had made. Baggy shirts with high collars, dark colors, hunched shoulders, and zigzag patterns. She leaned forward, resting her forearms on her thighs, and looked down at her new, deep cleavage.

Marbles

In a medium sized town in the Midwest, a little girl was playing with marbles when a clear blue one got stuck in her vagina. In that same town a third-grade girl got up to get a glass of water in the middle of the night and heard her parents talking about the vagina marble girl, who was in first grade. The third grader's parents were drinking white wine, which they occasionally did after she went to bed. She didn't mind that they woke her with their loud voices because, on those nights, she discovered the gossip she didn't yet have outside access to.

Until that point, she was unaware of the other hole between her legs. She stood in the doorway and listened to her parent's conversation until she understood. The third grader was a quiet and easy child. She observed without being involved, a fly on the wall. So this moment was one no one would ever know about. It would be three years before her mother would give her the illustrated book, *Where Did I Come From?* about penis and vagina intercourse and babies, followed by its sequel, *What's Happening To Me?* the puberty version.

The third grader went back to her bed, got under the covers, and closed her eyes. But she did not sleep. She bent her knees and placed her right hand between her legs, between the other two holes, and found the hole that seemed about big enough for a marble.

In the summer going into fourth grade, her friend Rose began to have daytime parties at her house while her parents were at work. Rose's older brother babysat from upstairs in his room. Downstairs, the soon-to-be fourth graders sampled clear liquor, vodka and gin, easily replaced with water, from the liquor cabinet.

One sunny afternoon, after multiple swigs of something clear and bitter, the third grader picked up a small square quilted pillow off the couch and placed it between her legs, positioning a stiff corner up toward her crotch, and said, try this. She rubbed the pillow back and forth between her legs. Her small drunk friends laughed and complied.

A few minutes later, Rose's brother came downstairs. He looked at them from the kitchen, smirked, and took a long drink out of a two-liter soda bottle. The almost-fourth graders froze. The brother shook his head and laughed. The girls stopped laughing. None of them knew the word *shame* yet, but they could all feel it in the heat of their cheeks.

The doors were hollow

Her parents were teen pregnancy young. We met in junior high when we were eleven.

Her mom was twenty-six. My mom was forty-two. Not a gray hair on my mom's head. My mom looked twenty-six. But my mom could have been her mom's mom.

Her parents were strict but looked cool. They had tattoos, smoked cigarettes and pot, and wore leather vests. Her dad rode a Harley and called himself *Dago* because he was Italian and proud of it, which I didn't know was derogatory until I was much older.

Like how I call myself *Jew* and *Dyke*.

Jamie was the oldest of three girls, all tough and scratchy voiced but small and pretty. She had wavy white blonde hair, big blue almond eyes, perfect round lips.

They had a lot of cousins around and listened to house music and stole make-up from Walgreen's.

They lived down the street in a row of old apartment buildings made of crumbling beige brick and stray cats. Two and a half rooms in their apartment. Jamie's bedroom was the half room, an enclosed back porch. No heat but private. Her parents had the room at the front of the apartment. The two sisters shared the other room, which you had to walk through to get to Jamie's back porch room.

Even behind doors, yelling in a small space takes up all the space. There was a lot of yelling at their house. The doors were hollow.

We smoked too many Newport cigarettes in the summer. Jamie wanted new mascara and Walgreen's was a short bike ride away. I had two dollars and forty cents. She wanted blue eyeliner, shiny pink lip-gloss, mascara, blush, sparkly eye shadow. She didn't ask for my two-forty. I didn't offer.

I saw her do it. Shove all of it into her bag. I pretended not to see. She was tough and cool, and I wanted her to know I was too.

Okay let's go.

She walked fast out the front door and I followed. My heart was beating quick, clammy blood around my chest.

Fuck fuck fuck shit.

Hey you stop! A security guard grabbed Jamie's skinny arm.

Let go.

Let me look in your bag.

I was frozen. I felt like throwing up. He took her bag.

Did you steal something? What am I going to find? he said.

She stared, quiet. He looked at me. I looked at the ground. He opened the bag then called in on his walkie-talkie.

I got them, he said. Come with me.

You too, he said to me.

I wanted to run. But I was too scared and too small to know that if I ran, I would get away. And in the core of my gut I knew I shouldn't abandon her.

When you're that small you don't know how it really works. You don't know that there's not much they can do. You imagine your life in jail, your parents hating you, never eating ice cream again.

He took us back into the store, up some stairs into a small office. Two other security guards and a store manager there. Our tiny bodies in metal folding chairs, their enormity looming over us until we shrank down to the size of the lip-gloss brushes we stole. They yelled we shrank they yelled we shrank some more. They told us we had to pay for all of it. They said every time something gets stolen they lose money. They threatened calling the police and asked if we'd like to spend some time in jail. They told us what we did was illegal, a federal offense, a horrible horrible thing. And then, they called our moms.

My parents were at work. Jamie's mom came to pick us up. I never saw her mom smile. Not once. Her eyes always red with a rage I knew nothing about. Maybe no one did. We waited for her mom outside the store. Didn't say a word. I could see Jamie was scared. More scared than me. I knew when my mom found out, I'd be grounded and yelled at. And that would be it.

When her mom pulled up, she barely put the car in park before she jumped out, slammed the door, and started screaming.

What the fuck is wrong with you, you little cunt. Get in the friggin car. NOW.

Her mom looked at me. Fire eyes.

She hated me. But even at eleven I knew her hate was there long before I was.

I can ride my bike home, I said.

She growled, threw Jamie's bike in the trunk, and got back into her car. As they drove away, I could see her arms waving and Jamie's skinny arms covering her little blonde head, curling forward.

The other kind of witch

Once there was a woman who was tapped into her capital "S" Self. She got regular massages, made herbal medicines and vision boards, and believed in the universal power of energy to manifest reality. She called herself a witch. But you couldn't tell by looking at her. She didn't wear pointy hats and long, black gowns. Her skin wasn't green and she didn't have any warts, save for the small one on her left big toe, which she removed with pressed garlic. She was the other kind of witch.

The witch had strong feelings about the downward spiral of humanity but was a generally positive person. When she was no longer able to bear a child, she felt free. Though she was not a child-hating witch, in fact she loved children, she chose not to have any of her own. The witch was saddened that, while there were so many unwanted children in the world, people continued to conceive new ones.

On a breezy October morning, the witch woke from a dream in which she found a laundry hamper full of babies. They were alive and smiling, reaching their chubby arms up to her. She picked them up one-by-one and lined them up in a row.

Where are your parents? She asked them.

You are, they said. You. They pointed at her and she began to cry.

When she woke, she vowed to cure the dilemma of parentless children in the world.

She put on her fuzzy slippers, grabbed a basket, and went out to the garden. There, she collected seeds from the Cosmos that had begun to dry up. She harvested the green tomatoes that wouldn't have a chance to ripen, half rotten turnips left in the dirt, overgrown Lemon balm leaves, and a few dried Echinacea flowers. She cut the sunflowers that were not yet dry but had lost some petals, two jalapeño peppers, a Mullein leaf, a Black-Eyed Susan flower, some grass clippings, and a handful of Chaste berries. She also took a few sprigs of mint for her morning tea, and an apple off the dwarf tree out front, for her oatmeal.

Back in the kitchen she set to work. She boiled water for the mint tea and started cooking the oats for her own breakfast. She pressed dried seeds and flower pods, herbs and fruit with the side of a butcher knife. Everything then went into a cast iron Dutch oven along with a pinch of this and a scoop of that from her apothecary jars. She salted the whole thing and cooked it on low heat for seven days. During the week while her brew baked, she sat each day with closed eyes and thought about the changes she would bring to the world. *No new children should be born until each uncared for child was loved and housed.* After each sit, she wrote her thoughts on onion paper and put them into the Dutch oven, where they soaked and burned into a potion.

At the end of the seven days, the moon was new, completely black, un-seeable. She took the pot into the dark woods behind her house and dumped its crisp contents onto the wet earth. She covered it with red and yellow fallen leaves.

Over the next month, news broke. Pregnant woman began to miscarry at all stages of their pregnancy. Woman who had already birthed children effortlessly could not get pregnant. Fertility clinics boomed with business. The front pages of newspapers around the world showed pictures of woman at clinics and hospitals in miles long lines. Doctors searched for answers, diseases, infections, bacteria, viruses. Scientists conducted studies on woman who had suddenly miscarried. In the western world, people blamed immigrants for bringing curses and diseases. In the East, people blamed women for being careless. But the doctors found no explanations, and the scientist's studies were inconclusive.

The witch watched as the world grappled. She was saddened, again, with the state of humanity. She went to the woods where she had emptied her potion and sat thinking about the next step. Now, she thought, if people could stop blaming each other and obsessing about their genetics, if people could recognize what family really means, her vision would become whole. She cried tears of hope into the decomposed herbs.

One year passed. The New York Times published an article claiming that the world had become infertile due to global warming and pesticides. People argued over the reason. Religious people claimed demons and homosexuality. Scientists and doctors, again, came up with various hypotheses, like invisible bacteria and viruses. Still, the world grew accepting of the phenomenon. Fertility clinics became abandoned and sperm banks closed.

The foster system began to thrive and many fostered children were adopted. Babies of all ethnicities were sold on the black market and stolen in the night. And though kidnapping hysteria rose, less children remained homeless as people became aware that they would never have babies of their own. Once the adoption centers were empty, people turned to homeless youth shelters and cleaned them out.

As the years passed, the babies that were once adopted, grew, never having known a world with babies or children. They never asked where babies came from. They never learned about birth control. They grew in mixed race households, never wondering why they didn't look like their parents, because most people had similar homes. Woman who had chosen not to have children were no longer harassed and frowned upon. There were no longer kids to go hungry, to be abandoned and abused, to cry on airplanes. Pediatricians retired and the whole specialty dissolved. The food and water crisis ended, as less and less people were alive.

On a breezy October morning, much like the one in which she made the first potion, the witch went out to the woods behind her house. She lay in her particular spot and covered herself with red and yellow fallen leaves. She closed her eyes and slept until her body composted into the dirt that was once a pile of herbs and wishes.

Redhead

She walked by at eleven-eleven on Tuesday morning. I saw her through the living room window, her orange hat bobbing in time with her feet. The following Thursday she walked by again. Same time, eleven-eleven. Same orange hat, bobbing. It happened again the next Tuesday and the next Thursday. Then again the following week. At first, I didn't check the clock to see if she would be timely. I was looking out the window anyway, drinking coffee.

After a month of watching her walk by at eleven-eleven every Tuesday and Thursday, always with the orange hat, she started to notice me. The first time she looked at me I squinted my eyes, pretending to be looking at something far away like a bird or a tree branch. She kept walking and I could feel her eyes shift away quickly. I was relieved.

That same week it happened again. She looked without slowing her walk. I thought she might, so I stood to the right of the window instead of in the center where I usually stood. I could see her orange hat bobbing a block away, before she could see me. When she got close I crouched down, only able to see her from the eyes up. She turned her head to look. I don't think she saw me.

The next Tuesday I decided to be bold. I stood square in the center of the window with my red mug full of coffee and a dash of cream. I planted my feet firmly on the floor, a little wider than I normally have them. I took a deep breath and imagined a long, heavy dinosaur tail reaching down into the ground from the base of my spine. I tried to relax.

I waited.

By eleven-twelve I started to worry. Eleven-thirteen, eleven-fourteen, eleven-fifteen. No orange bobbing hat. No eyes.

Maybe she was hit by a car. Maybe she had the flu. Maybe she lost her hat and had a breakdown and couldn't leave the house. Or maybe she didn't need to go wherever it was she went all those Tuesdays and Thursdays, anymore. Maybe I would never see her again. I went to the kitchen to finish the crossword, but I couldn't concentrate. There was an ache in my chest, like my sternum was broken. I didn't cry but I wanted to.

On Thursday of that same week, I went to the window. I did my regular routine, standing in the center with the red mug steaming between my hands, waiting. It was eleven-o-nine. I didn't look down the block to anticipate. I just waited, looking straight ahead. At eleven-eleven she walked by, bobbing orange hat and all. I was so relieved I almost dropped the coffee. My mouth and cheeks smiled. She didn't slow her walk but turned her gaze toward my living room window. I was looking at her. She was looking at me. Our eyes met. She was not smiling.

The world slowed down. Instant replay slow motion. Our eyes stayed locked, her head turning back, mine turning to the side to follow her. She looked away first because she had to. She was walking.

The following Tuesday she walked by at eleven-eleven. I looked at her. She turned to look at me. This time she stopped walking. I was smiling again, and she still wasn't smiling. She just looked at me. Her eyes seemed confused and I wondered if she might be late, spending an extra minute looking at me. I didn't look away. Finally, she shook her head and walked away, a little faster, probably to make up for lost time.

On Thursday, she walked by the window at eleven-eleven. Her pace quickened when she walked by my window, and she had headphones on. She didn't look. I didn't smile.

The next Tuesday, I saw her walk by, but she was on the other side of the street.

That Thursday, the weather was warm and my roses started budding. At eleven-ten a green bicycle whizzed past my living room window. No orange hat. But I recognized the gray backpack. Her hair was orange too and flew behind her like streamers in a fan.

The next week the weather got warmer and it seemed she would be biking from here on out. I didn't smile at her anymore. There wasn't time. And she never turned to look in my window. It was too quick.

In May, when spring had decided to stay, she was gone. I waited to see her, like the last time, hoping she had just missed a day, a week, a month.

But she never came back.

The second week in July there was a crossword clue: *Lucille Ball, for one.* Seven letters, last letter D. *Redhead.*

I thought of her. How her hair was the color of her hat: orange. People called redheads don't really have red hair. I wondered if she cared that she might not truly be what people called her. Orange is its own thing. It can stand alone without red. Although I suppose it needs red to not be yellow.

I have brown hair. No color needs brown to not be something else. Unless it just wants to be brown.

Pressing the cabbage

The phone vibrated. It doesn't ring anymore. I don't miss ringing phones. Sudden ringing phones used to scare the crap out of me. Like when I clear my throat and my cat jumps and hides under the bed.

I was thinly chopping a green cabbage then heavily salting and squeezing it to break down the cell walls and get it juicy, when the phone rang. I mean, vibrated. I usually miss calls because the vibration is a low sound and I rarely have the phone touching my body. I don't know how to make the phone ring or make a sound louder than vibrate.

I'm not trying to be uppity or make a radical statement by not having the phone with me all the time, I just don't want to be tethered. The Big Brother quality is unnerving.

The phone vibrated. I missed it. My hands were submerged in salty cabbage juice anyway. That's another thing, picking up the phone. We don't pick it up anymore. We push a button. So I couldn't have pushed the green *talk* button. I noticed the change on the screen when I walked into the other room to get the ceramic crock to ferment the cabbage in. The screen on the phone read, *missed call, 1 new voice message.* I don't have the kind of phone that automatically shows who called. You have to push a few more buttons for that information.

I transferred the cabbage from the big metal bowl into the ceramic crock and placed two ceramic weights on top of it, pressing them into the shredded cabbage until the juice came up over the top. It has to be fully submerged otherwise whatever is exposed will oxygenate and rot. I pushed and heard a satisfying fart sound, put the ceramic lid on top to keep bugs out, and tucked the whole thing into a corner of the kitchen counter. I washed the bowl, the knife, the cutting board, wiped down the counter, and swept the floor. I like to be barefoot in the kitchen, so sweeping always happens. I wiped my hands on a purple dishtowel, now covered in salty water and small chunks of cabbage. I took the towel to the basement and set it in the laundry basket of dirty dishtowels.

I studied myself in the broken mirror that sits next to the washer beside the basket. My face looked tired and my hair, messy. Making sauerkraut is laborious. I turned on the utility sink and splashed cold water on my face, then pulled the hair tie out of my messy hair and ran my hands over my head, careful not to undo the thick curls with my fingers. I re-pulled my hair back and up into a pile on top of my head, re-wrapped the curls with the hair tie and headed back upstairs.

On the front porch, I opened my composition notebook. They say if you write by hand, as opposed to typing, there is a creative chemical that gets triggered, a synapse between the brain and the body. Ten to twenty minutes or longer if I can't stop. On this sauerkraut-making day, I went for a half an hour, until my shoulder flared, and my wrist became tender. Sometimes the body is the stopping point. I put the composition book away. The cheapness of a composition book provides freedom to write whatever crap comes out. Speaking of crap, then I had to crap. A good writing session is like a morning cup of coffee. When the crap was over, my wife was home and it was time for external connecting. I forgot about the phone.

You don't have to open your eyes to see at night

Once we arrived at the bar called *Night*, everything changed. The air sounded like water and the lighting was warm and ambient, the way I like it. Ambiance is the most important part of any situation. It creates the mood, like the music in a movie. I care less how food tastes at a restaurant and more about the way the space feels.

At the bar called *Night*, everyone was dancing even when they were standing around sipping drinks, talking, or pissing in the corner. We were the bartenders, us looking in the mirror behind the bar like Mary Poppins harmonizing with her own reflection. And we smiled at each other for no reason. The conflict was gone, dissolved, forgotten. Like we were in a blackout but not drunk and sick. Just revamped.

At the bar called *Night*, we smiled at each other for every reason. We held hands and walked a loop around the place, our feet sticking to the beer stained floor, crackling with each step in a satisfying way. The past was a dream we couldn't remember and the people were all parts of you and me and the *us* we make together.

At the bar called *Night*, the bar hardly existed. Our skin dripped from our body frames as we walked, then our muscles, then our bones and we were everything. We were the air and the beer and the candles and the kissing. We dissolved like sugar into warm water.

And then, at the bar called *Night*, for a moment I remembered the last time we weren't together. We were in the same room, but in opposite corners. The lighting was fluorescent and there were no other people. No music. No hands to hold. No heat. The memory arrived but was too weak to sustain itself. I brushed it aside and you hardly noticed. You hardly noticed so I didn't say anything.

Chipped

On our second date, my grandmother died. Actually, that was supposed to be our first official date. We'd had burritos the week before. But neither of us was sure if that was a date.

On that second date I called to cancel. I was too sad. You understood.

In the morning there was a note on my car windshield with a dried flower attached.

You are loved. Feel good.

That convinced me I wanted to have a second date.

A month later we were in love. We had sex in the car, in your bed, in my living room, standing up, in the tub, in the garden, in the kitchen when no one was home. We made out all the time. You cooked eggs and broccoli for breakfast and made thick, strong coffee. Black for me, cream for you.

We stared at each other. You told me your dreams.

You never asked about mine. But I didn't notice.

Two months in, we went south to work on your friends' farm. We worked hard during the day and drank beer and whiskey at night. We laughed all the time. I loved being in love with you in front of everyone.

One drunk night you got angry. Out of nowhere. That's the way it always went.

You got drunk got angry yelled at me. I wouldn't fight. You got angrier.

Let's talk in the morning was my line.

You don't love me was yours.

I went to sleep in the car. You followed me to the car, opened the door, yelled some more and slammed it hard.

You didn't look like you. Your eyes changed from milk chocolate to black.

After that I slept in the car a lot.

Your stepfather raped you every night until you were nine.

You couldn't tell me what your triggers were. You didn't know so I couldn't be careful.

They would just appear, and you would regress.

Tantrums like a toddler.

I don't want to be like that, you said.

I held out for a year. I loved you.

We went to therapy. The therapist told you that you were manipulative when you mumbled because it made me have to lean in to hear you. To come closer. To care.

The therapist said you didn't listen to me. I told you I loved you just like that: *I love you.* But you never heard me.

We filled out a test form: *What is your partner's favorite book? What does your partner dream about? How is your partner's relationship with his/her family?*

I knew all the answers for you.

You knew none for me.

I was surprised.

But not really.

When I got sick you gave me herbs you grew in the garden. Tincture medicines you made in your kitchen. You drew hot baths and rubbed my back. You drove me to the airport and held me when I cried for no reason. You took care of my cat when I was out of town and you cancelled plans to be with me. On my terms. You gave me control.

And that was how you showed me love.

One night, you came to my house to help me pack. I was moving to a new house the next day. We drank two bottles of red wine. And then I realized drinking was one of the triggers.

You started crying. Hard. Out of the blue.

I held you for an hour. You talked about him. What he did to you at night in your bedroom. Nighttime scared you because that was when he came in when you were a child. When everything was quiet and dark. Your mother in the next room. She did nothing. She didn't believe you. No one did.

I stayed holding you, talking you down. *He's not here. He's not coming here. It's over.*

But I was never able to change your mind.

Your emotions escalated. We went outside to get air. I put your bike in my car. Told you I would drive you home. That you'd feel better in your own space with your cat and your stuff.

You wouldn't let me drive you. You said you would ride.

I pulled the bike out of the car.

Okay I said. *You need to go then.*

You refused.

You screamed.

You don't love me. You don't care. How can you tell me to go?

You pushed and finally, I got angry. I had to finish packing. I had to sleep. It was almost midnight and I was worried you would wake the neighbors. That someone would call the police.

I told you again to go. I went inside and locked the door. You tried to get in. You screamed through the windows then crawled in through the half-open cat window.

I went to the bedroom and locked that door. You slammed your fist against it and screamed *fuck. FUCK.* And then you went home.

The next day you called. And called. And called. I was moving. I had no time.

I had no patience left. I told you I would not see you again if you didn't get therapy immediately. At least three times a week. And quit drinking completely.

You did.

And for a minute, things got better. Until you ran out of money and the therapy stopped. And the whiskey and beer returned.

When things got bad again, I made boundaries. I wouldn't see you. For a while, I hated you. For pushing me away. For telling me I didn't love you right.

For having an experience I was lucky not to have had.

And for knowing too many people who have had it.

Amnesia is best

The blonde is hunching her shoulders forward. Her eyebrows are lifted, creasing the space between her eyes. The brunette is hugging her knees to her chest. They are sitting face to face on a Fir bench in the backyard where the blonde lives. Overgrown grass creeps behind the bench and Soba, the skinny old-lady cat, is sitting in the shade of the brunette's body. The sun is bright, but the air is cool. Summer has not quite arrived. They wear short sleeves anyway. There are goose bumps on the brunette's brown arms. The blonde's arms have begun to turn pink.

I'm not in love with you, the blonde says.

The brunette reaches for her coffee mug. Before she brings it to her mouth, she looks at it. It's empty, save for the bitter mud at the bottom. She tilts her head back and lets the mud slide onto her tongue, swallows, then places the mug back down on the bench beside her.

I have to pee, she says.

The blonde forces a smile. The brunette goes into the house through the back door, to the bathroom. While pissing, she notices *The Little Prince* on the floor beside the tub. The book is wet. It bothers her that the book is always on the floor in the bathroom. She has thought this many times.

When her bladder is empty she sighs, wipes, pulls up her jeans, and walks out the front door. The blonde hears her go but says nothing.

The SUV was too big and the man behind the wheel was too distracted with his phone to see the blonde on the bicycle. The moment of impact was just so, a perfect T, perpendicular the way chaos and nature line up on their own. Destiny was a theory the blonde did not believe in.

The bumper of the car pressed into the center bar of the bicycle and lifted the blonde off her seat. She rolled onto the hood of the car and into the windshield, spraying blood and glass in all directions. Her helmet cracked down the middle.

The man sat looking at the girl lying in the street in front of his car through a web of cracked glass. He did not move. The girl in the street did not move either. The car was stopped, and the front bicycle wheel spun like a bug on its back waving its legs.

When the ambulance arrived, they lifted the blonde carefully onto a stretcher and loaded her into the vehicle.

Are you all right? an EMT asked the man.

The man continued to stare through the windshield. He said nothing.

She's going to be okay, the EMT said.

The man hung his head and began to cry. The EMT touched his shoulder.

The man drove his SUV to the hospital and waited to hear news about the blonde's condition.

Broken femur, broken wrist, and three cracked ribs. And she has amnesia, the nurse told him.

Maybe she won't remember what I did, the man said to himself.

What happens is quick. One moment changes everything. Even after it's over, when you didn't realize it changed anything. Even though you don't know the future, a moment is a switch. The switch of a face in the linking of eyes that turns your perspective when you don't notice, from the outside. But as soon as she looks at you, you can't see anyone else. A spell. A hook. Nonconsensual hypnosis. It's never chosen and it always hurts. And from the beginning, from the moment you didn't see coming and knew nothing about, what you do know is that she will reach into your chest barehanded no gloves and pull your sweaty heart straight out, cracking the breastplate on the way. She'll squeeze it, ring it out, spit on it and pull it apart like string cheese. And you'll watch having known having done nothing to stop it without having given permission. Then she'll give it back one aortal section at a time. You'll piece it back together inside the cavity and you'll cry because you won't be able to fit it together like a puzzle. The pieces won't click.

I never loved you, she'll say and you won't understand because when she looked at you the day you met and every time after that and even in the moment of I don't love you, you were inside of her and she was inside of you.

You know it's impossible to have that without having it.

You fed her pink grapefruit from your mouth. She squeezed your ribs and kissed your neck while you washed dishes at two a.m. after the party. She said you made her peaceful. She said your bodies fit perfect and tight. You won't understand and you'll start to wish you had never met her. You'll wish you were someone else so you could run her over and give her amnesia. Then she'd forget she didn't think she didn't love you. And then you'll wish you were her so you wouldn't remember that she doesn't think she loves you.

Quicksilver Kevin Bacon

There's a place you can go in the winter, when it's too cold to go outside or when you hit a spring storm, full of underground tunnels and above-ground glass walkways. The gravity there is different and if your timing is right, you can find younger selves of celebrities drinking beer, like Footloose and Quicksilver Kevin Bacon.

I was riding my bike uphill to the north. A spring breeze tangling my hair and the sun baking my face, when, in a turn of events, I hit a snowstorm. Biking uphill in the snow. These things happen. Sometimes it's better to choose south.

When I hit the storm, I turned my bike handlebars sharp to the right and, at that moment, found an entry point. It's not hard to find a way in, you just have to know it's where you want to go. I leaned my bike against a dark interior wall and started walking. I didn't know where I wanted to go, but I didn't *not* know. I was just going, following the path toward the lights and the people noise. I found them around the first corner.

Younger Kevin and some other younger-self famous guy I knew I should recognize but didn't. They were drinking beers and talking. Younger Kevin winked and smiled at me and I felt my face turn hot. I kept walking. I walked down the dark path, alone and quiet breathing in the musky air that dwells in tight cave-like places. I walked without expectation, but I knew something would happen as the noise grew louder and the lights brighter. What I found around the next corner I would not have anticipated.

A huge glass ceiling under which was the biggest bar I've ever seen. It looked like a mall, though no one was shopping and there were no stores. Just people drinking at tables in the middle and around the edges, all lined with bars. A mall, an airport, a fishbowl. I was overwhelmed. I scanned the place right to left, left to right, right to left again, up and down, then turned on my heals and walked back down the narrow path toward younger Kevin Bacon. The quiet path wrapped my body and made me breathe harder. I tried to walk past them without looking, so they wouldn't think I was noticing them. They noticed me trying not to be noticed. Kevin didn't say anything out loud, but I heard him, in my head, telling me to turn around. When I turned, he wasn't looking. I started walking back to the mall-bar and in a moment of confidence I said, I'm just going to get a beer. Younger Kevin said, yeah do it.

I took that to mean I should get a beer and join them. So that was my plan.

Back at the mall-bar. Everything open, people everywhere, no one familiar but the overwhelm starting to wane. I walked toward one bar and ordered an IPA that never arrived. I stood. I waited. I small-talked with the other people in line. Time felt slow, like I had been waiting forever. I started to panic that younger Kevin would be gone by the time I got my beer. I looked up at the glass ceiling, snow falling toward me, sun shining through the snow, wondering how snow can fall and sun can shine at the same time. My eyes hurt from the brightness, but I didn't look away. I breathed in deep the smell of beer and cold. As I exhaled, something left my body. Something I didn't need. What I felt in my body was, fuck all of it. Fuck waiting for the beer that will never come. Fuck caring about younger Kevin who is the epitome of my insecurity and fear of failure. Fuck trying to get anywhere or be anything according to anyone else.

I took in another breath and held it in my lungs, my core stretched like an overfilled water balloon. With that breath, my body floated up off the ground for a second. When I exhaled my feet landed without a sound. I took another breath and jumped. The breath lifted me higher and I floated in the air longer. I kept jumping, leaping, breathing until I became a helium balloon, weightless, slow in control, hovering, stretching my legs into split leaps. People around me smiling and clapping and shouting, do it again! and, look at the air dancer! I jumped higher each time, hovered longer, stretching my legs farther, until my feet no longer came back down.

My body lifted up to the ceiling. I pressed my palms against its cool glass. Another breath. Another. Another and the weight of my hand pushed open a glass panel. I smelled the cold air, sharp through my nostrils, the sun hot on my face again. My body grew toward the hot cold sun snow and swam into the sky.

The house on the hill

My friend rented me a house on a hill. Not exactly on top of the hill, but on the slope, so the house was tilted. Aside from being on the slope, the house was its own block in the middle of three streets that formed a triangle. I've never understood this design, being in the middle of things with no corners, trapped and all alone.

The inside of the house was magnificent. Everything was oak and maple wood, the walls, the floors, the ceiling, like a cabin. There were skylights and bay windows, letting in all the available sunlight. The beds were made up in brand new crisp purple and white sheets, and there were two queen beds per room. The second bedroom was sunken, so it felt like another wing.

Perfect for privacy, my friend said.

Still, I wasn't sure I wanted to stay there. Not in the house and maybe not even in the town, for no clear reason. My indecision dragged out. There was a nagging feeling in my bowels, which, as it happens, were unobstructed. My philosophy is, when you don't know what to do, it's best to do nothing.

Time lapsed and as I continued to do nothing, my friend decided to rent the house himself with his two kids and his mom. Even when you do nothing, something happens, often by someone else's hand.

As soon as he moved in, I felt regret for *not* moving in. But it was the kind of regret that you feel when you know you made the right decision, when you didn't do something because you didn't want to disappoint someone. And, maybe things would have worked out if you'd made the other decision.

The decision was made.

My friend was happy, and I cried because I was leaving town and would miss him. I had no home and no destination. The only way to do something without doing anything is to make a grand adjustment. My friend said he'd miss me.

I'll miss you too, I said.

But he didn't cry. He was already onto a new life in a beautiful sloping cabin of a house.

Landlord

The landlord is outside her window drilling into some sort of metal. The ruckus is too loud to ignore. She would like to go outside and drill right through the landlord's head. But not because of the noise. She would like to drill through the landlord's head because the landlord is a jackass. Not a jackass because of the inconsiderate drilling, but just a jackass because of general inconsideration.

She would also like to go outside and take the drill out of the landlord's dirty hand, set it down on the workbench, unplug it, and take the landlord by the arm into the house. She would like to take the landlord into her bedroom to be thrown down on the bed where she might hold down the landlord's wrists and put her mouth to the landlord's full lips. She might tie the landlord's hands to the bed frame with a scarf, pull up both of their shirts, and kiss some more.

Or, she might not tie the landlord's hands to the bed frame. She might leave them free in order to feel the landlord's hands move around her skin, her ribs, her ass, and inside of her. Maybe the landlord would throw her on the bed and pull down her pants. Maybe *she* would go outside to get the landlord, but the landlord would lead her inside and tell her about wanting to taste her.

She'd like it if the landlord would just decide the loud metal drilling was done for the day and would come to her door alone. The landlord might knock, then come in with force, make a joke they'd both laugh at, and kiss her standing up. Maybe the landlord would push her up against the door and they would rub their bodies together that way.

But the landlord *is* an inconsiderate jackass. The landlord comes over to work in the workshop and tells her about the difficult girlfriend, that they are trying to split but the girlfriend won't have it.

Then she and the landlord flirt, she asks the landlord in, and the landlord refuses, unavailable. She knows this. The landlord knows this.

But they continue the charade.

I had a dream our faces were touching and I could smell your breath, she says.

I had a dream we were kissing and bound together with fishing twine, the landlord tells her.

The landlord continues to drill throughout the week. She would like to go outside, take the drill from the landlord's hands, and throw it on the ground. She would like to then smack the landlord hard across the face, saying she cannot be inconsiderate to the girlfriend.

She would also like to say that what happens between two people is private, that no one needs to know. She would like to live from her heart, profess her love, and not worry about how others might feel about it. She would like to go outside, unplug the drill, and go to the beach with the landlord where they might cook salmon over a driftwood fire and talk about the meaning of life. Then, later, they would

go back to the house, take their clothes off, and fall asleep to
the sound of the neighbor's wind chimes.

You lived across the hall

I kept seeing you from behind. The back of your dark curly head, closing your door just as I was opening mine. Romeo and Juliet started that, the split-second timing of missing someone. Ships in the night. None of us actually lived there. It was just for a month. Art camp. All of us there for our own separate reasons, together.

There was the night of the party in our corner of the building. Twenty-year-olds drinking red and orange neon mad dog in round plastic bottles. The rest of us beer to bourbon inside a cloud of pot smoke. Everyone's door was open. Sticky hot Colorado-in-July summer air. You were standing between our doors in a group. Everyone shouting over everyone. You said, hi.

I've seen you around, I said.

You smiled. I smiled. Drunk and stoned. A conversation started about making out.

If you want to make-out with someone, I said, you have to just tell them. Who cares?

You laughed.

I went to my apartment and you went to yours. The party continued. An hour later I was in your cluttered kitchen trying not to notice crusty cereal bowls and dried soda stains on the counter.

We should make-out, you said.

Okay, I said, tomorrow.

Then I left, smiling to myself.

From the back your hair is short, tight tight black curls close to your head up into a square shape. It's gently greasy with a grease that doesn't absorb into my skin but sits in my palm, the way oil and water don't mix. The first time I touched your head was when I was fucking you in my temporary bed. I wiped my hand on the white starched pillowcase. After I fucked you with that hand, I wiped it again on the same pillow and, through the dark, saw a stain.

I think you're bleeding, I said.

Oh thank god, you said. I had a pregnancy scare last week.

The next day after the party, I was working at the dining table alone, my roommates out doing whatever ladies do on Saturdays. I had the blinds drawn. It was too hot for me to go outside or let any of the outside in. You knocked. I wasn't sure if you were you or the blonde across the hall in the apartment next to yours. The neon-mad-dog-drinking-twenty-year-old who was so butch under the surface of her little girl dresses and long Barbie doll hair. Every time she opened her mouth, a deep baritone came out. I had told her the night before, at the party, that she seemed gay.

I swing both ways, she said. Then she smiled real butch-like without looking away.

Come in, I said when I heard the knock. It was you.

Aww you're working, you said.

You were impressed. I played it cool.

Come in sit down, I said and closed my notebook.

You sat next to me at the table and turned your long legs in my direction. I sat back in my chair. You talked about a boy you were moving to Vancouver to be with. I let you talk, and I listened. And then there was another knock. The blonde.

Come in, I said and both of you were there in the living room.

I have to crap, I said.

Wait give me your number, you said.

Then you left gracefully, claiming you were supposed to go hiking with friends.

The blonde stayed, awkward, and said nothing. She waited until I was done in the bathroom, and then I gave her a haircut. The night before I had boasted about my fancy haircutting scissors. I sat her down in a plastic chair in the kitchen, asked about her family, and got bored. Sometimes the fantasy is better than the action. Sometimes.

I have to get back to work, I said and she left.

When you got back from the hike, we saw each other in the hall.

Come over, I said.

I took your hand and led you upstairs to the room with the starched white sheets. No transition into the next moment, tangled on the bed, your red lace panties stuck between my fingers.

Nice, I said.

You laughed and said, take them off, pushing my hands down, sliding the lace along your thighs.

Fuck me, you said. So I did.

That's when I touched your hair and found your blood
on the pillow.

A breastless acquaintance

What I understood was that my breasts were full of cancer and I was going to will it away. That's what I told her, the woman who no longer had breasts. She wasn't my friend, just an acquaintance, sitting in front of me on a soft wooden bench overlooking the lake. It was something I had always known, that I was full of cancer. I've always had fibrous breasts. My mother and her mother and my mother's cousin all had breast cancer. The cousin died young.

I knew people would think I was crazy for not having surgery and radiation, like my mother and her mother. My aunt died because she did nothing. But I was not going to do nothing. I always knew if it happened to me I would not go to an allopathic doctor. I knew I could think it out of me, the way I did with a toothache once and that sciatica I had down the back of my left leg, with yoga and tinctures and visualization and candles.

I had my first mammogram when I was 39, at the vagina clinic. That's what we called it, my wife and I. Everything in the clinic was pastel pink and mauve and there were giant flower paintings framed in more pastels on every wall. The vagina clinic. No men were allowed behind the big, pink, vagina door because all the women getting their breasts squeezed and radiated were walking around in robes.

My wife heard a robed woman whisper to one of the nurses, There's a man in here.

Her eyes darted toward my wife, who was wearing a snap back cap and saggy jeans.

That's not a man, the nurse told her.

She told me this story when I came out of the boob-smash room in tears. The story dried my tears. We laughed.

My tears were not from the physical pain of the stern radiologist pushing my head to the left while she squeezed my boobs around to the right. They came from a deeper place. The tears came from the sting of being disconnected from my mother's pain, my grandmother's loss, my aunt's fear. They came from knowing I have to do it differently, to break the cycle, the deep grooved habit we have been circling around since our language was more guttural.

I felt afraid of what my mother would say about my decision. She believes in the tarot card readings I do for her. She drank the tea I mixed from plants in my garden when she had her own cancer, and she used the herbal salve I made on her radiated, burned skin. But she also had surgery and toxic drugs and so many mammograms. I thought of not telling her. I thought of not telling anyone and just letting this breastless acquaintance hold my secret. I thought, if anyone else knew, the cancer would have power to grow. If I gave it nothing, it would die.

How the rain sounds when you put the gun down

We rented a cabin in a state park up north. Nothing fancy, just a hard twin bed, a rocking chair, a small electric heater, and some nice looking old wood for floors and walls. And of course, a porch. I'll do anything for a porch. If you want me to do something for you, build me a porch and the favor is done. The cabin was on a lake and it was windy and cold and magical.

On the second night we were there, rain. So we sat in the rocker eating bread and cheese, watching the rain fill up the lake, listening to it pour down like clapping hands. No other sounds. Until, a knock at the door. I wanted to ignore the knock, but that seemed like the wrong thing to do. I got up and looked out the small window of the wooden door. There was a beige state trooper hat attached to a tall man with darting eyes. I ignored the instinct telling me not to open the door, because of the hat. Maybe he was here to relay a storm warning.

I opened the door. The first thing he did was take off the beige state trooper hat. He dropped it, or threw it, or the wind picked it up and it was gone. Then he ran into the cabin. He pulled out a small generic gun, like the guns in movies. I don't know about guns. It was just a regular silver handgun. He pointed the gun at me, his eyes still darting like he was high or scared or both. I sat back down in the rocker. We both sat and rocked while he pointed the gun at our faces. He said nothing. We said nothing. He was shaking. Two three four minutes passed. Then he put the gun down on the table. Not to surrender. Just to adjust his pants or get something out of his pocket or take a bite of our bread. He looked down and my body jumped up and grabbed the gun. No thoughts. No words. Just me and a gun, like Tori Amos. Me and a gun. I pointed it at him, and he said the first words any of us had said up to that point.

He said, you don't know how to shoot a gun go ahead and try to shoot me.

First of all, he was two feet away from me. Second, before we came to the cabin, I had been watching a show about the KGB in the eighties, which was full of gun play. In one episode, an FBI agent showed his co-worker how to shoot a gun. I paid attention. So I was not feeling entirely inexperienced in that moment. Plus, the adrenaline.

I was pointing the gun at him, not looking at him, but looking through the hole at the top of the gun, like the FBI agent had said to do. I was looking through the hole and I took a deep breath and pulled my finger back to push a bullet out.

He was right about the first bullet. I thought it went through his shoulder, but I missed. I was two feet away. I missed. He laughed. I did it again. And the second time, it went through his throat and it went through his body and I kicked him in the nuts, and he fell to the floor. But instead of the loud thud his body should've made when it hit the old wooden boards, his body shattered into tiny pieces, like a ceramic plate. Tiny dust. I sneezed. The dust, that was once the fake state trooper, flew into the air and out the open door into the night, into the lake. I put the gun down on the counter and we went back to eating bread and cheese, listening to the rain.

Jewfro

This morning, her hair was kinky curly, Jewish. She tried to run her fingers through it, but they got stuck at every bend. It was big. Much bigger and longer than it had been yesterday, full of tiny loops. The kind of hair she'd always wanted. Hair she even thought that she deserved, seeing that she was, in fact, Jewish. Even though no one thought she looked it.

Yesterday, her hair was much shorter, with a little more length in the front. She wore her bangs swept to the side and, though her hair wasn't kinky, she still called it a Jewfro because it was frizzy, thick, unruly. Usually, she oiled and flat ironed it.

At first, she thought someone had put a wig on her head while she had slept. She went to the mirror and studied it. She wove her fingers into the sides of her scalp and tried to pull up, thinking it might come off. But as she did this, she could feel where the tiny curls grew out from beneath the skin of her head. This made her smile. Things do change overnight, she thought.

It wasn't that she had been praying for this kind of Howard Stern hair, or even thinking about it lately. But it was in the back of her mind to try and grow her hair out, to see what it did, maybe curl it when it got long. Alas, here it was. She ran her hands under the weight of her new hair and gave it a flick. She wanted to feel the wind in it.

The sun was shining, and her bicycle sat beside the house ready for a ride. For the next few hours, she rode around town feeling the air coil around the spirals in her hair. The feeling made her laugh. Someone shouted at her, Shabbat shalom! Then someone else, Good Shabbos! She didn't live in a Jewish neighborhood. When she got home, her friends had made matzo ball soup and a quiche for Shabbat dinner. They were just about to light the candles. This was the first time she had come home to Shabbat dinner.

Tea and death

It was a windy day when I found her hanging under the deck.

I walked into the kitchen to make a cup of Oolong. There was a creaking sound under the floor. I went outside, followed the sound, and found her with a bruised neck and a purple-white face. Her body was swinging in time with the leaves of the sugar maples. No one else was home.

The teakettle whistled so I ran back inside. I decided to make Pu-erh instead -- a special black tea infused with Chrysanthemum. An old friend brought it back from China. She knows how much I love tea. This one in particular is supposed to heal the stomach and strengthen digestion. I have a weak stomach. It's weak when I eat certain cold foods, like tofu. Not so much when I see things like blood, although I do get nauseous when I see slimy. I don't consider blood slimy. Slimy would be more like snot or that rubbery stuff in chicken.

Death is not slimy.

When the Pu-erh finished steeping for three minutes, I went back outside. The wind grew stronger and the sound of her body swinging changed in rhythm. I wondered if her neck would snap and she would fall to the ground. This might be slimy to see and my stomach might weaken, so I decided to walk the other way into the woods. The air was warm, and I heard some crows yelling at each other. Crows don't sing, they yell or talk or caw. There were no other bird sounds.

The Pu-erh was strong and hot in my mouth. It felt good going down my throat and I could tell my stomach was being healed and strengthened as I drank.

I love walking in woods with a hot cup of special black tea.

I walked for another half an hour, listening to the dry maple leaves and branches crackle under my boots. I thought about calling my friend to come over for a cup of Pu-erh but then thought against it. I wasn't sure if the swinging under the deck would bother her and I didn't want to take a chance that it would.

Never mind the color

I met Patricia Clarkson at a craft fair where I was selling handmade books for a friend who makes them. Patricia Clarkson, the redheaded actress. She approached my stall in her casual way, as if she didn't care that she was famous or didn't care if anybody else cared. I acted cool and she asked how much for a brown leather covered book.

We made eye contact when she handed me the money for the book and she said, you would make a great redhead.

Then she slipped me a small scrap of paper with a phone number and some other numbers scribbled on it and told me where to go to make it happen. I nodded.

The next day, I found myself sitting at a long farm table in a hair salon amongst a few other people. I didn't know anyone there, but they were all as charming and friendly as Patricia had been. I hadn't realized how long my hair had gotten until everyone at the table started talking about it. They were all in awe. I might have blushed.

A receptionist, or maybe she was another stylist, or both, came over to the table and stroked my hair the way hairdresser's do, assessing it. She told me it would have to get bleached before I could become a redhead, that the process would take a very long time. Patricia came over and agreed, saying it would take two whole days: one day for bleaching, the next day for the color. I felt like I was forgetting something, like I had somewhere to be. Like, how could I spend two days getting my hair done? I felt anxious but I didn't want to say anything because this was Patricia

Clarkson. Patricia Clarkson, the cool German artist in High Art. Patricia Clarkson. And she was really doing me a favor. As if she could feel my panic through touching my hair, Patricia smiled at me with her whole face, her squinty, mysterious eyes beaming into me, and I realized there was nowhere else I had to be.

She took me up some eighties art deco stairs and sat me in a chair. She stroked my hair the way the other woman had and talked to me like we'd been friends for years. It was comforting. I like when I don't have to say anything to fill the space. She took a wide flat iron and pulled it through a piece of my long hair. As she pulled, the hair turned blonde. I watched in the mirror, surprised.

I thought this was going to take all day sitting around with tinfoil wads on my head, I said.

Patricia laughed her throaty laugh and said, no honey this is how we do it now. Isn't it amaaaaaazing?

She did my whole head in less than ten minutes, long bleached blonde hair through my fingers and around my shoulders.

When the bleaching was done, she said, aren't you just famished? Come on.

She walked me to another table and asked a shorthaired woman for a tall stack of tiny pancakes with apricot jam and butter.

Eat up, she said.

Some of the people from earlier came to the table to eat the tiny pancakes with us. They all said my hair looked fabulous. I asked Patricia for her email address. I always ask for emails because I like to write to people. Nowadays, you're creepy if you ask for someone's home address. She said she had ten different emails so she gave me a few of them along with a code to give to the building guards on my way out, so they wouldn't be suspicious of me. Since she was famous, she had to be extra cautious with people.

My hair was bleached blonde and we didn't talk about the next phase into redheadedness. I guess she thought it looked good as it was. I didn't ask and I was glad for my new look. I just wanted to stay in touch with Patricia Clarkson.

Left hand and a dream

She watched the river pass beneath them as he drove them over the bridge. The passenger side window was streaked, she noticed, and dirty like the river. Then she looked at the shiny ring on his left hand. She thought it strange how the ring didn't show the wear of the years it held. And she thought about how he probably missed his wife, and how she missed her partner, even though, here they were together, smiling and happy, a vibrating coil between them thick as the twelve years it held. He left work early for her. They drank stouts in the middle of the day.

She looked again at his hands on the steering wheel. She thought about how thick they've grown since they'd both become adults. How his face was full and his demeanor softer and more open. But his eyes like youth, the same as always. Sparkly girl eyes. They talked about the day they met, all the times they fucked, all the people they remembered but have lost touch with.

The next morning she wanted to call him to tell him about the dream. How he left his front door unlocked for her to wait inside until he got home from work. His wife had set a dozen white plastic bags full of something soft on the counter. She cautiously touched the bags the wife had left and felt squeamish. Fish, she thought. Some of the bags started floating around the kitchen. The kids weren't there and there were candles lit all over the house. The house was otherwise dark, and the candles didn't make shadows.

Her friends came over and they drank wine on his couch. She couldn't tell if the wine was red or white because she couldn't see it, and the flavor was dull. His wife came home before he did. The wife was eight feet tall like in a funhouse mirror and wearing a red dress. She felt nervous to see the wife, but the wife hugged her and told her she was making him a romantic dinner. The wife wasn't angry that she and her friends were there in her house. In fact, the wife didn't seem to notice anyone.

She poured her wine from a round glass into a tall bottle to take home and suggested to her friends they leave. He came home just as they were leaving. She felt uneasy and he was distant. Even though they hadn't physically touched. Not since he'd been married. He never would. Not even in her dreams.

Tender splinters

The next day, you weren't there. I knew you wouldn't be after our phone conversation the night before.

My position, you said, overlaps my own skin with uneven threaded stitching.

My bones, you said, are ductile and my soft spot has not yet hardened from birth. We do not share a blood type. We intersect at the fork and choose contrary. I have been sewn together wrong.

I knew why you said what you said. Still, insecurity protruded, breaking the thin skin of my chest. Shards of flaking bone. Unseen splinters tender to the touch.

Everything can be logical if you stay above the neck. Everything can make sense. But the heart never rises above fragile clavicles. It stays in its little cave surrounded by flat breastbone and scar tissue, always bleeding on the inside. We are always naked under our clothes.

The heart is a liar.

My heart tells the truth.

The heart holds thoughts. Not the thoughts you decide, but the thoughts you don't hear. They travel down between cracks of bone where jelly marrow and blood run hot. They circle stem cells and run with oxygen pumped from lung cilia, little interior tornados protected by ribcage rods. They seep into thin fiber casing. And there, they turn into saccharine.

Bones are lighter than steel and stronger than concrete.

You didn't come because you got lost. You have a bad sense of direction. Not on the street or in the woods, but of which direction to choose.

Your feet listen to your mind and find their way. But at the T your heart doesn't listen to your feet or your mind.

You didn't come. You look forward too far, laser eyes, better than 20/20 vision. When your sight is better than better, you don't have to squint. The words are loud behind your sturdy teeth. I hear them under my nails. I need to clip my nails.

The end of the earth

I rode my bike all the way to the water, which was the end of the earth. The bike ride was downhill the whole way and I could feel the wind whip around my scalp between the hairs. I had big, long hair.

When I got to the water, I rode my bike right into a boat dock enclosure. Through a small glass window at the far end of the boat dock, I saw three men sitting in an office. I think they saw me, but they didn't seem to care that I was there. Out the side door was water as far as I could see, sparkling in the sun. Lake Superior, or an ocean.

I looked down into my hands and found a pile of shiny diamond rings. I didn't know where the jewels came from, but I knew we had a lady clan, with big, dark hair and the feeling of being bigger than we were. We were jewel thieves. I thought about how I never thought about being a jewel thief, how I don't even like jewelry, and I don't watch those kinds of movies. But then, here I was in a jewel thief gang of two, me and you, unafraid and slightly reckless.

I looked again into the window of the office to make sure the three men couldn't see my stolen goods. I wasn't scared. I put the rings in either of my coat pockets and felt their weight tug against my sides. The men didn't see me. I was hiding our secret wealth and it felt good.

It occurred to me that I had to go back because I was alone, and I wanted you there with me. I wanted you to choose the ring you would wear. But the bike ride was steep uphill, and the wind was strong. I panicked for a second,

until I realized you would wait for me, even though you
didn't know where I was.

Messy

I dreamed she had AIDS. In the dream, someone told me, and I crumbled to the floor, sobbing. I caught the saltwater in my hands and it was thick, sliding down between my fingers like clear molasses. My hands looked distorted through the water. It felt good to cry. It's been a long time since we kissed.

In the dream I called her on the phone, and she laughed, denying it. But I knew she was lying. And then she was there, standing in front of me, looking down. I was sitting on a rock. I hugged her jeans around her waist and breathed in. She put her hands on my upper back and, even though I couldn't see her, I knew she was smiling.

The lie didn't matter against the comfort of her body.

When I woke, I thought about how AIDS is not as big a deal as it used to be. It's 2014. There are drugs. People live long, seemingly healthy lives with AIDS these days. Not everyone. But a lot of people. Especially in the western world. Then I realized I was awake. I opened my eyes all the way and took a deep breath. But I still wasn't sure she was clean. I called her.

She said, no I don't have AIDS thank you for thinking of me.

Then she said, I'm going to inpatient rehab. So... close.

I told her I would write her letters and visit on Sundays. She asked why. Because she wanted me to say I care. I did. Say that.

The next day I proposed we have one more meeting.

When you dream someone is sick or dying, the feeling leaves an unwashable residue under your skin until you see them and feel their health. I disclaimed understanding if she thought it would be too messy to meet.

I hope it's messy, she said.

The things you left

I.

The first thing I found was a white long john shirt. While I was making the bed, the day she left. The blankets were tangled from sex and the way she sleeps, tossing and whining, wondering if I should wake her up this time, if this is a bad one.

The shirt fell from the bed in slow motion. When it reached the ground, it curled into a ball like a cat squeezing into itself. I bent down and kissed it and whispered, good night, stroking the collar, taking in the smell of her from the armpits. The shirt seemed to fall asleep. I continued making the bed, conscious not to step on the shirt. I fluffed the pillows, placed them side-by-side, smoothed out the comforter and went to work.

When I got home that evening, the cat and the shirt were asleep together, spooning in the same spot the shirt had fallen asleep before. I got into bed. The cat woke and jumped into bed with me, so I lifted the shirt to join us. I didn't want it to be alone on the floor. I hugged it, smelled it again and thought of her lying next to me. I would not return the shirt, even though I would see her every Sunday and I knew she would ask me to bring it. Along with the candy, the gum and cigarettes that I would sneak to her under the outdoor lunch table when no one was watching. I would avoid talking about the shirt. She would forget about it anyway, because of the weight gain and because she had so much to do, between groups, earning coins, and fighting for a place in her new home.

2.

After I made the bed that first morning, I found her toothbrush on a shelf in the bathroom mirror cabinet. It was lime green with a pale blue stripe down its belly. I hadn't really looked at it before, so I picked it up and introduced myself. Its bristles were sharp, erect and clean. It was still a baby.

This was not the first of her toothbrushes that had lived with me. There was one a few months ago, a purple one I got free from the dentist, that I gave her to adopt. That one only lived with me for a couple of weeks until we temporarily broke up and I threw it away. When we got back together, I apologized for getting rid of it.

She said, don't tell me tell the toothbrush.

I imagined that young purple brush in a landfill somewhere and I sent it good vibes.

I examined the green toothbrush, turning it between my fingers, poking its sharp hairs into my palm. I didn't want to throw it away, to make the same hasty mistake I'd made last time. But she would be gone for three months and I was pretty sure she already had a new one. I was hesitant to break this news to her old brush. It was too young. And yet, the cabinet was small. I could really use the space.

That night when I got home, before visiting the cat and the shirt, I went to the bathroom. I brushed my teeth with my own toothbrush, a brown handled recycled thing with a replaceable head. The green brush looked like it had rolled over in its spot on the shelf. I picked it up, said hello again, and walked toward the garbage can. I wavered, then put it back on the shelf before I could say, goodbye.

3.

At the bottom of my laundry basket I found a pair of gray boxer brief underwear, size medium boys. I put them in the wash with the rest of my clothes and forgot about them. The next day, as I was folding my own underwear and tube socks, the boxers came out static cling stuck to a white towel. I pulled them off the towel, the sound of ripping paper. I thought I heard cries. Both the towel and the underwear needed independence, and I told them so.

I smelled the towel. I smelled the underwear. Fresh. I folded the boxers, then unfolded them. They'd be happier next to the shirt still lying in my bed, in the spot closer to the window.

I let the underwear rest just below the shirt stretched out in its natural shape, allowing a breeze to easily pass through the legs. I tucked the bottom of the shirt into the elastic waist of the briefs so that they could get to know each other, even though they were already familiar, familial.

The clothes looked small and flat lying in my bed. They didn't fill up the way I wanted them to.

I didn't tell her about the underwear. I knew she would feel guilty for leaving the pair behind. Also, though I don't think she would say this, they were useless to her there. She knew they would no longer fit.

The food was starch, and the few vegetables, canned. I would eat lunch with her there on Sunday's. Eat not eat. I couldn't stomach it. Thin grimy coffee, dirty pale salads. I moved unidentified yellow mush around a beige plastic plate, so it seemed like we were eating together, being normal. I pretended not to notice the tough tattooed and scarred men glaring at us. She was the only outwardly gay person there. There were other gay girls, but none of them had girlfriends that came to visit every week.

The weight came as she got used to the food. She was self-conscious about her new body, saying, I told you this would happen.

I said, I don't care you still look good to me.

We both got used to the staring. People got used to her. They started asking her questions and soon she became a cool, tough girl who could hang in the workout room with guys by day, and gossip with girls in their bunk beds by night.

I didn't keep the shirt and boxers in my bed for long. It's strange to sleep with unoccupied underwear, especially ones that aren't yours. They ended up folded neatly at the back of my own underwear drawer. Eventually, they would turn into cleaning rags and, after that, trash.

4.

I found a nail clipper in the dryer after washing a pair of pants she left in the basement. The pants had been sprayed by a cat at someone else's house. She stayed at a lot of different places; I couldn't keep track. I never found out whose cat sprayed the pants. She didn't know either. I washed them with a load of my clothes. I never keep a nail clipper in my own pockets, so when I found it, I knew it was hers. Mine lives on a shelf in the bathroom not far from the toothbrushes. I always know where it is. She never really lived anywhere, so the nail clipper, among many other things, had to live as a wanderer in pockets, place to place.

Her nails were always a little rough. Cut tight and cracked. She didn't drink enough water. And in the rare times she did have a job, it was working with her hands. It wasn't that she was too high to hold a job. It wasn't even about that. The rhythm of her life was chaos. She never had a job long enough to keep a place to live, or she never lived anywhere long enough to keep a job. Something would happen, her brother would get arrested or her mom wouldn't have enough money to pay the rent, so she gave them the little money she had. The madness was so familiar that it was a relief to her. If nothing happened for long enough, she would find a reason to quit her job or move.

She worked for a landscaper for a month, digging dirt and planting trees. She washed windows and did dishes at diners around the city. Before she left, she painted cars, which was the most toxic. Once, she came into the bar I was working at, after her shift, looking like a coal miner. She'd taken the bus all the way across town with her clear plastic safety goggles on her forehead and a ring around her eyes like a reverse raccoon. Her blonde hair looked gray and when she kissed me, I tasted paint. She stayed until the end of my shift and I fed her drinks until she could smile again. Then I took her home to a shower and put coconut oil on her hands.

I let her put her hands all over me, no matter what shape they were in. I liked that she always had a nail clipper on hand and that she kept her nails short. It felt good when she scratched my back.

I took the nail clipper to my room and sat on the bed. I held its weight, lifting my hand up and down like you do when you're trying to feel how heavy something is. It had some weight. I squeezed so its mouth opened and closed.

How are you, I asked it. You must have had quite a time in that dryer.

No response. Nail clippers don't have much to say, I think. They live a long time, so they are more mature than even the oldest toothbrush.

I wondered what to do with it. A nail clipper is an in-between thing. Because it's metal, it seems okay to share. But there can be blood and fungus, so maybe not a good idea. She wasn't allowed to have anything sharp or metal in there. Too much of a tool or a weapon. I wasn't sure how she was supposed to cut her nails, so I made a note to myself to ask her on Sunday. But then I forgot and never remembered, because her nails didn't seem to get very long. I ended up putting the clipper in a drawer in my closet. It disappeared. Probably left quietly in the night to find a better, more useful life.

5.

On the dining room table in a mason jar used as vase, were red and white tulips. They were fresh a few days before she left. She always brought flowers. Every time she came over, except for the one time we were in the middle of a fight about nothing. Always about nothing. The fights all bleed into one after a while and you forget what you're fighting about. It was the same fight over and over again, both of us stuck in our own patterns.

She usually hijacked flowers from someone's yard. I liked the bouquets she made. Even though she didn't know what she was picking, she ended up picking useful herbs, like yellow Saint John's Wart flowers, or orange Calendula. I would tell her what they were and put them in old beer bottles with water. I told her she would get caught one of these days, that it wasn't okay to pick plants out of people's yards. She laughed, because she did a lot of illegal and more consequential things than taking flowers. I laughed too.

One day she came over out of breath with massive red Dahlia's, which you *really* don't pick out of someone's garden.

She said, I ran so fast because this old man came out of his house and started yelling at me for picking his flowers.

She was sweating and laughing, and I told her how cultivated and special Dahlia's are.

Thank you, I said. You're my hero. But don't do that again.

The tulip bouquet was different. She knew she was leaving so she scrounged up money, likely borrowed from her ex, and bought the flowers from the grocery store. The day after she left, they opened a little more. Then, each day the edges of their petals started turning brown and curling inward, like they were sad. One by one the petals fell onto the table, covering it with yellow pollen dust. The water in the jar became shallow and brown and the stalks hardened. I left the jar until I could no longer stand the compost smell, then dumped the whole thing in a corner of the backyard, like burying an old pet but without the burying. I tried to wash the jar, but I had left it too long with the nasty water and I couldn't get the brown ring out. It was easier to throw the jar away.

6.

There are leopard print covers on the front seats of my car. They get folded up in the crease sometimes and things get swallowed, like crumbs and coins. Sometimes, the shininess of something metal catches the sun and draws me in. A month after she left I found the sparkly switchblade, with the cream and brown handle, in the crease of the passenger seat while I was stopped at a red light. It wasn't a particularly sunny day, but something drew me to look at the seat. I reached my hand down to touch it, not sure what I was seeing.

Pssst, it said, I'm still here.

It was me who drove her that day, with her backpack, a pillow and two blankets. And it was me who wouldn't turn the car around when she said, never mind I wanna go back I can't do it.

I said, too late you have to you can do this.

She smiled and said, you're right thank you.

When we got there, we sat in the car in the parking lot and she handed me the switchblade and said, can you keep this for me I know they won't let me have it anyway.

I hugged her and said, yes leave it here.

I didn't notice where she put it because I went inside with her. I got out of the car first. She sat, staring at the building.

I said, come on let's go you can do this you can you can.

I pulled her bag and the pillow out of the trunk and told her to take the blankets.

She got out but said, no I wanna go back I can still go back, and I said, it's your choice but you already decided, remember?

She said, yeah oh yeah okay.

We walked in together and she said her name to the guy at the front desk. It felt like everything was going to be okay but I knew that feeling wouldn't stay after three months of visiting every week, of being watched like prisoners, nowhere to fuck or kiss or even hug.

I forgot about the switchblade, which she always carried in her left front pocket but never pulled out to use. I held it then, for the first time.

Open me, it said. I want to stretch out and be free.

I can't, I told it, I'm in the middle of driving. What if you accidentally stab me?

I would never do that, it assured me.

But I wasn't convinced. I put the switchblade in the glove box.

7.

The same day I found the switchblade, I found a small handful of unmarked pills in the console between the front seats of the car, amongst some gum wrappers and pocket lint. After the switchblade, I decided to clean out the car. I don't know how I'd missed seeing the pills for such a long time. I think they appeared when they were ready to be noticed.

The pills were pink and blue, tiny circles with a few blue and white cylinder capsules. They didn't look like ibuprofen or antihistamines. They didn't look like any drugs I could get at Walgreen's. They looked alive, like the guys on the street with greasy hair and unfriendly smiles who housed them. Or like the feeling I got when her friend, the one who went to jail for selling dope, came around.

When I found the pills, I did not say hello.

I said, get out. I shouted at them. Get! Out!

But they just lay there, passive like I couldn't make them do anything. I scooped them up in my hands. Some of them tried to jump out and hide under the seat, bury themselves in the carpet of the car. I scrambled until I got them all and went straight to the outdoor garbage can. I didn't say goodbye. I didn't say anything until the lid was closed.

Then I said, fuck, to no one. Just, fuck.

When I went to visit the following Sunday, I told her about the pills. Because I didn't remember her dumping them loose and free in the console and I'd only let her drive my car once, when I was drunk. She never had a driver's license.

She said, oh no you threw them away?

And I said, are you serious?!

Then she said, oh I mean sorry for that.

And I said, what the fuck?

Sorry, she said, sorry.

She said sorry a lot.

I didn't ask what kind of pills they were, and she didn't tell me. When I got home that night, I searched all the tiny places that pills could hide around my house: other pill containers, a tin with bobby pins, the backs of the cabinets in the bathroom and closets, the freezer. I didn't find any more pills. But I did find a syringe.

8.

There was a plastic sandwich baggy with a bunch of garbage in it, candy wrappers and old receipts all crumpled up, hiding behind a couch cushion. I heard it crunch the way paper and plastic do when you sit on them. I reached my hand between the back of the couch and its pillow. When I saw the syringe, I dropped the bag on the floor. There was no needle, just the plastic part, so I picked it back up.

I opened the bag and pulled the plastic part of the syringe out. I wanted to smell it, but I resisted. I didn't even know what to smell for. I held it the way you're supposed to hold a syringe and squeezed. It sighed in my hand, blowing out a small puff of air, like an exhale. Like it was exhausted. Then I pulled the base back out, making it draw a breath in. I heard that too. I let it exhale again. I put my left hand in front of the hole where the needle would go and pushed and pulled with my right hand, inhale exhale inhale exhale, a few more times, feeling the air on my palm.

The repetition was calming and, at the same time, the reality of what was in my hands turned from curiosity into anger. This might be the worst thing I found. Worse even, than the pills, because this was her main tool. She wasn't particularly into pills, so the pills didn't feel as threatening or as violent as the syringe. And the act of taking pills is something most people do. I didn't like to picture her cooking drugs and emptying them into that pea shaped bruise that lived in the crook of her elbow. I saw the bruise all the time, but I never saw how it happened. Toward the end, I started to look for more bruises. I measured the size of the main bruise with my eyes. Has it gotten darker? Is it healing? Sometimes she noticed me looking and said, don't look.

Sorry, I said and looked away.

When I was nineteen, I watched a friend shoot heroin in my bedroom. I didn't know she was a junkie until I'd known her for a year. Like my girlfriend, she was a functional addict. It's easy to not see what you don't know you're looking for. Or what you don't want to see.

When she asked me if she could shoot up in my room, I said, only if I can watch.

Aside from movies, I had never seen someone do that. I knew if I didn't let her do it in my room, she'd do it somewhere else, somewhere unsafe on the street. I also wanted to see what would happen.

She sat on my bed and I watched her from the doorway. She wrapped her arm in a large rubber band and said, wanna try? I considered it. I wanted the experience.

I said, no way I never will.

Watching her, knowing that was part of her life, didn't scare me. I didn't yet know the consequence.

I put the syringe back into the baggy and took it to the outside garbage can to live with the pills and the stinky trash. I tried to forget about it, but it called to me, muffled under the heavy lid of the garbage can, traveling up the walls, through the windows, and into my bedroom.

Let me out, it said, please.

I turned up the music.

I told her about the syringe the week after I told her I'd found the pills. We had talked on the phone the day before, which we sometimes got to do. She had phone privileges on Saturdays. Sometimes someone else would stay on the phone too long and she'd lose her time. Sometimes she'd try to call her mom, whom she rarely got a hold of because her mom often didn't pay her phone bill or was too high to answer the phone. But when she could, she'd call me.

We talked that Saturday before the Sunday I told her about the syringe. I didn't want to tell her over the phone. Fights happen too quickly without eye contact, and we only had ten minutes or less on the phone. I tried to keep the conversation easy. I asked her how things were going, if she was making friends, and she told me about her groups, working out with the tough guys, the shitty food. She told me she was making progress, that even though she was getting fat, which made her feel bad about her body, she was happy to be clean and have a clear head. She said the tough guys and the girls, who were also tough, were starting to respect her. They saw how she could hold her own, being the only gay person. She was one of the guys *and* one of the girls. An in-between. She felt proud and I was proud back.

I didn't want to shame her about the syringe. I knew she was trying to change, to be accountable. At the end of that phone conversation we said, I love you, like we always did, and then, I can't wait to see you tomorrow.

The next day was Sunday and I went to visit. Family group was in the morning. I was her official family while she was there. She said it was easier, that people would take her and our relationship more seriously if we said we were "partners," like real family. We sat in a room with a bunch of couches, like an AA meeting. Everyone introduced themselves and the family members said who they were there to support. Sometimes they'd cry. I never cried. I only cried at home when I was alone. I always said I was there to support her and that I was proud of her. Then someone gave a motivational talk and there was another go-around, if anyone wanted to add anything. I never added. After the group we went to the cafeteria, which was like a huge gym in a middle school and had lunch with pale brown coffee in beige plastic cups. Sometimes there was cream for the coffee. Everyone got excited when there was cream.

That day, we had lunch outside on a picnic bench. The sun was shining, and things felt good between us. She smiled a lot. I told her she looked hot.

After we ate, we walked around the track, the only place you could walk outside. Some people jogged to get exercise. The track was a big field with an oval dirt path, a quarter of a mile once around. We tried to sit on a log at the far end of the track, which butted up to the road, to talk. But we sat too close and one of the staff yelled across the track that we needed to keep walking and make more physical space between our bodies. This happened every time I went to visit.

The first time I went was two weeks after she'd gotten there. We were starved for each other. She pulled me into the bathroom and we made-out in a stall. For a moment, we were free. Then I got scared we'd get caught and she'd get kicked out. I didn't want to risk it. She knew touching wasn't allowed, but she wanted to take the risk. Because taking the risk was the most familiar feeling for her. She didn't think about the consequence, only the impulse.

We got up and kept walking and talked about how annoying it was that we were always being watched, we couldn't even hug or hold hands. I reminded her she wouldn't be there forever, that this was part of her recovery and it would be okay.

Then I said, I want to tell you something.

And she said, oh god what.

I said, it's not a big deal I just want to keep good communication.

I told her about the syringe.

She said, sorry, like she always said. What else could she say? I didn't expect anything else. I just wanted her to know I found it.

Then she said, I didn't shoot up at your house I swear.

Okay, I said, it doesn't matter.

9.

The food stamp card appeared on the floor at the foot of the bed. Maybe the cat had been playing with it and swatted it there. I picked it up. It was scuffed up and old looking, like it had been through the washing machine a few times. It looked dead.

I held it up to my ear and said, hello?

Nothing. I called the number on the back to see if there was any money left on it.

Zero, the machine said.

This was how she'd take me out to eat. We'd go to the health food store and get big salads at the salad bar deli. Then we'd get a little chocolate cake from the bakery case. You could buy everything with food stamps at the grocery store.

My treat, she'd say. And then we'd get ice cream to take home.

When she was really broke and no one would loan her money, she'd sell food stamps off her card. Once, when I was shopping at the grocery store while she was away, I made eye contact with a guy and I smiled, to be friendly. After that we kept seeing each other around the store. It didn't occur to me that he was following me until he approached me.

He said, hey I have food stamps and I need some money want to buy some?

He explained I would get more than the amount I'd give him, so that would make it worth it. I would give him cash, say fifty bucks, and he'd give me seventy-five on the food stamps card. I told him I didn't have any cash on me. He smiled like he understood. No one ever asked me that again. It seemed strangely coincidental.

When the food stamp thing didn't work for her, or when she didn't feel like bothering, she'd borrow money from two different people, which were essentially the same relationship. One was her ex-girlfriend, who had a kid and wanted to get back together with her. The other one was another girl with a kid who wanted to be her girlfriend. She slept on both of their couches sometimes and borrowed their money and their cars. She did their laundry and took care of their kids and complained to me about how they weren't good parents. She never paid them back and more than once she got pulled over in one of their cars without a license. Neither of them ever got mad at her or said no.

I thought about keeping the card for her until she got out, but she'd have to re-apply anyway and would likely get a new card. I threw it away. I didn't tell her. She didn't keep track of things like that. Nothing she owned had a permanent home.

10.

Everything about her was like high school. She still listened to Skinny Puppy, dyed her hair black, which was longer in the front, wore baggy jeans wide rolled at the bottom, black Doc Martins and crisp white T-shirts. She had a collection of white T-shirts. I found one behind the dresser not long after she left.

I had my own white T-shirts. Just two, and they were smaller. She wore her clothes baggy like a skater boy. When I found the shirt, I knew immediately that it was hers and that she wasn't missing it. She had clothes at all the places she "lived" - at her mom's house, friends' houses, in her backpack, and at my house.

She didn't want to leave things at my house because, she said, you and I are different.

I made boundaries with her that no one else made. She lived in an enabled world where she got what she thought she wanted. I wanted a healthy relationship. She didn't know what that felt like. But she tried.

I pulled the shirt up to my face and breathed deep. It smelled like deodorant and laundry soap. For as much as she moved around, she was obsessively clean. Her hands were always cracked because she washed them so much. She tried to keep her body and her clothes clean so that you couldn't see that she wasn't clean. I liked how her clothes smelled.

I brought the T-shirt when I went to visit one Sunday. I knew she didn't need more clothes, but I didn't want to keep it. Of all the things, I didn't want the T-shirt. It felt like the epitome of her. It was too clean, a farce.

After she was in there for a few weeks and her weight changed, I told her not to wear white T-shirts because they didn't look good. We were just that way with each other. We were honest. Maybe I was too honest, for the both of us, but she didn't seem to take it personal.

She laughed and said, I know I'm fat now.

And I laughed and said, you look cute I like it.

I was honest about that too. The day I brought the T-shirt was the day she told me about the times she wasn't honest.

She said, remember all those times you asked me if I was high because you said my eyes looked fucked up and I said I was just detoxing well you were right I was high.

I wasn't surprised. I knew it, even though all those times I had wanted to believe her. She was holding the shirt when she said that and we hugged and I felt the shirt on the back of my head and someone told us we were too close, and we had to stop hugging. Then we bonded talking shit about the assholes that ran the place.

I said, this sucks, and she said, it fucking sucks so bad.

I said, you can do it, and she said, I don't know if I can, and I said, I know you can I know you can.

She smiled and went to her room to put the shirt away and I went to my car and listened to sappy music and cried the whole way home.

II.

I found a wad of gum on the windowsill beside the bed the first morning she was gone. It was the first thing I found, before all the clothes, the pills and the rest. The gum was fresh, almost still soft because she had stayed with me the night before. I didn't hesitate picking it off the sill and throwing it away. I was used to touching her chewed up gum. But when I looked back at the window, the sill seemed naked.

She chewed gum partly for the sugar and partly because she smoked all the time and was self-conscious about her breath. When she was done, sometimes she'd put a chewed wad on the dash of my car. Not because she was saving it for later, even though she said she was, like that girl in Charlie and the Chocolate Factory. She always forgot about it and then I'd forget too until I found it later. I could tell when she was going to leave a wad somewhere and I would give her a sideways look like, don't you dare. She'd laugh and wait until I wasn't looking, stick it somewhere. It was disgusting. I tried not to be judgmental. I never got outwardly mad at her about it. It was funny. But toward the end, it moved to the pile of things that annoyed me.

She'd ask me to bring gum on my Sunday visits. Gum was contraband, so I had to slip it to her under the table. But if you were already chewing it nobody said anything. I always brought gum.

12.

The thing she had from the beginning to the end and long before we met and likely even still, was the raised pea shaped bruise in the crack of her left arm, just inside the elbow crease. It looked like it hurt, like a cooked split pea. I noticed it every time I saw her, even when I wasn't trying to. It jumped out at me like it wanted me to see it, like it might start talking to me. I didn't know what it would say, but I imagined it had a lot on its mind.

I was repulsed and fascinated by it. I'd sneak looks at it when I thought she wouldn't notice, mostly to see if it had changed. I used it as a marker of what she was doing, to see if she was lying. When she noticed me notice, she'd move her arm out of the way and tell me not to look.

Once, I asked her why it wasn't changing and she said, it is look it's smaller.

I couldn't tell. It never looked different to me. I wanted it to, but it never did.

I started to look for the bruise in the crook of my own elbow, forgetting sometimes my elbow wasn't hers, the way bodies become fluid when you're consistently tangled in someone else's. I'd rub the insides of my arms and look at my protruding veins.

She said, you have good strong veins, and laughed.

I didn't find this funny. I didn't think any of it was funny. But I laughed with her so she wouldn't feel alone. It was good that she was able to laugh about it. I wanted to make light of it. Though I always thought about the bruise, which made me feel desperately sad.

13.

I found one dirty gym sock all alone without its counterpart, behind the dresser in the closet. It was white but so dirty that it barely looked white. She wore two pairs of socks year-round. This made me feel crazy. I don't like socks in bed and the thought of two pairs of thick gym socks, one sock atop the next on my foot, makes me feel like I can't breathe. I don't like layers. I don't like nail polish or scarves. I don't like feeling suffocated.

She said, my feet are cold and also they stink.

This was true. Her feet smelled like a men's locker room. She thought two pairs of socks would help. It didn't.

There were so many socks all the time everywhere. Four socks for one use. And there were also my socks, similar in style. It became difficult to tell which socks belonged to which feet.

The dirty gym sock I found behind the dresser was not the first. I often found stray socks bunched up in a corner of my house. But that last sock was the only one she left behind. It was like a lost child in the grocery store, scared and sad and alone. Though I didn't want to touch it. I could see how bad it smelled. I pinched it between my thumb and first finger at the cleanest looking edge and held it at arm's length from my body. I walked through the house and to the outside trashcan.

Sorry, I said, you gotta go.

I didn't feel bad about my decision. It was dead.

I spent the next month wondering if I would find its pair.

I never told her about the sock. I kept forgetting about it when I saw her. Leaving socks behind is not like leaving a syringe. The sight of the bruise, which did start to fade after a couple weeks of her being there, belittled all the objects.

14.

A hickie is a bruise but not the kind of bruise like the one on her arm. The hickie she left me with was intentional and the process of receiving it was the point. It was part of the way everything started between us. This one was yellow and in the shape of her mouth. It sat right in the middle of my chest between my tits and hurt to the touch. I liked the feeling. It was like the tulips, a little old but still tender and alive. Both meant not too much time had passed.

By the time the hickie was completely healed, a lot of things would have changed.

Mostly, I was the one who gave the hickies. I liked the feeling of her flesh between my teeth, like biting into a chunk of Brie cheese, soft and salty. I'd bite her shoulder and upper arms, her neck and her tits. Occasionally, things switched. I liked being on the receiving end too, to feel equal. Things were often not equal. When we talked about the world, how we both deeply loved animals, we were uniform. When it came to our day-to-day lives, she was living in chaos without a ground.

A recovered addict friend said, people date addicts because next to the addict they're the one who always has their shit together.

The first time I went to visit her, I tried to pull down my shirt in the front enough to show her the hickie. They were all watching us all the time.

I said, push right here, and I put her hand between my tits.

She smiled.

She said, push right here, and she put my hand on her shoulder.

I looked at the hickie between my tits every day. I pushed on it and each day it hurt less and less so I pushed harder and harder, until one day it was gone, and I felt nothing.

15.

When you're in recovery, you get metal or wooden coins every time you reach a landmark in being sober. You get one at the one-month mark, two months, six months, a year, five years. Each coin is a different color and has some inspirational quote, like the serenity prayer, written on one side and the words, unity service recovery, around a triangle on the other side. A number marks the time, like a two in the middle of the triangle, for two months. The coins are meant to inspire people to stay strong and sober and to honor the hard work of getting and staying clean.

She didn't have any coins when she first left. She didn't go to meetings at all at first, which is where you get coins. But while she was there, all she did was go to meetings. Meetings were mandatory. She lived there for three months, so that's what she did. They gave out coins when folks reached certain points in their time there. When she got her first one for one week of sobriety, she was proud to show me.

I held the coin between my fingers and turned it around to see all the details, feeling its gentle ridges. I felt proud too. It was shiny golden yellow and a little heavy, like it was worth something.

She wanted me to keep that coin and all the coins that followed. I think she hoped she would eventually have a huge collection, the first thing she'd followed through with in her life. She gave them to me as they came to her, because I was the person in her life who wouldn't lose her details.

She said, can you keep this for me so I don't lose it?

I felt honored to be the keeper of the coins. I put them on my altar in front of two white candles and touched them every day. And every week when I went to visit, she'd say, do you still have my coins?

When she first got out, she went to meetings all the time. She had momentum. She collected more coins from those meetings and added them to my altar. They shined gold red blue and silver next to the candles and made me feel hopeful for change and growth. They were worth more than money. They were a struggle won. They were victory and the emotion that victory inspires.

She said, I think I found a sponsor I think I found my home meeting I can do it I am doing it.

I said, yes you are you're amazing.

There was a feeling of joy and success and beauty. I told myself I made the right choice staying with her.

16.

There are thick metal screws with loops on the ends, attached to the four corners of my bed. Through the loops are wide nylon ropes, their ends tied off with black electrical tape. I gave her money to get the hardware and she rigged it up. We started with her holding me down and shifted into using props. I bought a book on Japanese rope bondage. She called her friends that were into kink.

First, there were shorter ropes connected to the bed.

She said, put your hands together like you're praying, and then wrapped one of the ropes around my wrists. Then she said, spread your arms out above your head, and tied each wrist individually.

In the book we saw a picture of a women with a rope woven intricately around her torso, from the neck down to the crotch.

That one, I said.

Yes, she said.

I gave her more money and she bought fifty feet of the same soft nylon rope.

I took off my clothes and put on tall black boots. She draped the rope around my neck and evened it out. She hardly looked at the picture in the book. She was good with her hands. She wrapped it front and back around my body, tying knots and looping. After an hour she was done, and it was beautiful. I looked in the mirror. I was a macramé basket. She took a few pictures. It was hot. No one had ever tied me like that before. I felt close to her, like I could be with her forever. We spent the rest of that night fucking. And for the next few weeks, we looked at the pictures and talked about it every day. She showed the pictures selectively to her friends.

I said, don't show everyone.

She said, trust me I'll only show my close pals.

I felt shy about people seeing, and also proud. It looked like art and she said I looked sexy. We talked about learning more ropes ties, maybe going to a workshop. We fantasized about doing a lot of things, like going to the mountains, camping, Europe, the beach. But we never did any of it. She never had enough money and more than that, she would never make a real plan and commit. After the initial excitement, the ropes fell to the floor and stayed there, collecting dust.

17.

It's not really chapstick. It's organic lip balm in a small plastic tube that poses as chapstick. In the time we were together, I bought her at least five. She never got halfway down a stick before she'd lose it. Too small of an object to keep track of.

A tube of lip stuff generally lives in a pants pocket, which goes into a washing machine. Or in a backpack, falling to its bottomless pit. Or put down on a bathroom counter, only to fall to the floor and roll into the corner behind the trashcan or the toilet. The world is a lip balm vortex. Even I, who rarely loses anything, have lost many of these.

The first time I went to visit, I tried to think of all the things she needed and wanted but likely didn't have. Lip stuff was at the top of the list. She used to ask to use mine, ruby pomegranate flavor. Her lips, like her hands, got particularly cracked in the winter. I didn't feel it when we kissed though. I loved kissing her. I bought her a ruby pomegranate lip balm.

She was happy and I said, don't lose it, and she laughed and said, I won't.

But I knew she would. A lot of things got lost in there, "lost" being stolen. She told me about a girl who stole from everyone, and everyone knew it. There'd be confrontations, which turned into fights, but she never admitted taking things, even after the stolen things were found in her room. Nothing in there was safe. Too much trust given to people who are unfamiliar with how trust works. Nobody had a sense of permanence. Not with objects and not with emotions. Personal walls shifted all the time, breaking down in intimate and emotional moments in group therapy, then going back up as soon as no one was there to hold that kind of space. I knew not to bring her anything I might want back, like books or CDs. I knew, even before she was in there, that anything I gave her would likely never find its way back to me.

I found the lip stuff in my closet under the dresser. I put it on a shelf in the closet, thinking I would use it when the one in my pocket ran out. It sat quietly, never a sound from falling over or calling out. Nothing.

I forgot about it.

For a period after she left, I paid more attention to things. We didn't get as tangled as some people do but she always left something behind, as an anchor.

When things were hard between us, she'd say, I'll stop by to grab my things, or, when should I drop off your books?

Objects were a way to have an encounter, to make one more emotional connection. Tangling objects is a way of hugging without touching. Especially when an emotional boundary is made. It's a way to hold on. It's comforting and it made me feel like I was real, like our relationship was real.

18.

When we met, her hair was dyed black and shaved on the sides. But it changed often. And she wore a lot of hats. Hats weren't allowed inside so she only took one hat with her, the trucker cap, to wear on walks in the field or on the basketball court outside. In a couple of the pictures, she's wearing a gray newsboy cap that she wore regularly in the beginning of our knowing each other. She looked good in any hat. The bowler hat added another nineties element, like a Goth Debbie Gibson.

She didn't wear it often. It was reserved for fancy occasions, which we didn't have many of. There were times she tried to make our hangouts together fancy by dressing up in a crisp white button down and clean black pants, polished black boots, washed hair, and the bowler. She would show up at my house smelling like men's cologne with a bouquet of flowers, freshly picked from a stranger's yard. In the beginning, she talked a big game about getting her shit together. I liked it. She liked to fantasize. You don't know until you're with someone long enough if they will follow through.

We never went anywhere when she got dressed up. The bowler ended up on the arm of the couch, then found its way to the floor under the couch, to collect dust. A lot of her things collected dust at my house.

I found the hat just before she got out. By then I had convinced her to let her hair go back to its natural color, blonde light brown. Someone's mom, who was a hairdresser, offered to cut it in there in the beginning, to get all the black out. By the time she got out, her hair had started to grow into a shaggy skater style, bangs swooping to the side across her face. The color made her skin look richer instead of the pasty look that happens with black hair against fair skin. She looked healthier because of it, and also because she was healthier. When she got out after three months, I realized that was the longest she had been clean in the two years we'd been together. I had been a participant in enabling the illusion. I let her lie to me because I wanted to be in control of the truth.

When I found the bowler, I dusted it off, put it on and looked in the mirror. I looked ridiculous but it made me excited for her return.

I'm sorry you have been so neglected, I said to the hat, be patient she's coming soon.

I twirled the hat around my finger, then hung it on a hook behind the door and said hello to it every day after that, until she returned.

19.

When I first start dating someone I write a lot of letters, even when we are not apart. Letters are a way of talking when there's no other way.

When she decided to leave, I said, I will write you a letter every day.

She said, that's amazing I will try to write you back.

Try was enough of a commitment for me. It didn't hurt my feelings that she couldn't say she would write back for sure. I knew there were other things she needed to focus on. I also knew that she would write me at least once. She could get excited about anything for a few minutes.

There are a handful of letters. They're like those greeting cards you open and a song plays. That's how they sound when I read them. They talk to me. And also, they look like some of the letters I have from when I was a teenager, words in all capitals, each letter of each word overly structured, like she took time to make sure her penmanship was exact, the way you do when you're not confident in your writing. All the O's have a diagonal slash through them, like zeros. The E's look like old English. And the words take up a lot of space with their bigness, as though they are more important than their meaning. They are short all smooshed together and say things like, *I don't have a lot of time but I'm doing okay I love you*, and, *can you bring me a poetry book and some gum can't wait to see you on Sunday*. Mostly there are letters on white paper in white envelopes, but there's also a postcard with a Buddha drawing on it. On the back she wrote, *I didn't draw this but I colored it in*, and, *I miss you I love you*. I pinned the postcard to the wall above my desk.

20.

By the time she got out three months later, it was May and the air was warm. There was a graduation ceremony in the cafeteria gymnasium. Lots of families, little kids, and friends. I showed up alone but a separate crew of her old friends also came. To everyone's surprise, her mom came too.

We sat together in a huge circle. Each graduate was called up to the center one-by-one to receive a coin and a diploma. Something nice and funny was said to introduce the person and then the person said something nice and funny about the hardship they'd endured in their life and the struggles they overcame while they were in there. She said she was thankful and committed to getting her life together. Everyone said some version of that. Then the person sat down, and each family member had a chance to say something. Her mom cried. I didn't say anything, and I didn't cry. None of her friends did either. We told her how proud we were later, in private. I just wanted it to be over, the ceremony and the entire experience. I didn't have any tears or even the emotion that tears come from until much later, when I was far enough away.

After the ceremony we all went to a vegan restaurant. Her mom, whose eyes and hands were unnaturally shaky at the ceremony, was not invited. She already needed space from her mom. When she was a teenager, her mom would kick her out of their one-bedroom apartment weekly, in sudden bursts without reason, sometimes in the middle of the night, hitting her and screaming. She'd go back home a few days later and her mom would cry and tell her how worried she'd been.

She was happy that her mom came to the ceremony. Her mom told her she wanted to get clean too and could she help with that. She said she was hopeful, and she believed her mom would try.

That's great, I said.

She nodded and smiled.

I knew that was just a moment suspended in time, alone, motionless. She knew it too.

At the restaurant we went to the bathroom together and she said, thanks for coming all I want to do is go home with you now.

I said, me too it's almost over and then we'll go home.

We kissed and held hands under the table through the dinner. We ate vegan eggrolls and mock duck with broccoli and fried rice and then I put her bags, pillows and blankets in my car and took her home. The weeks that followed were the best.

She moved in with her old friends, the ones that came to the graduation, also in recovery.

I wanted her to move in with me, but she said, it's too good I don't want to ruin it I'm not ready.

We decided to wait until she got settled, in two or three months. I'd go to *her* house and watch movies in *her* living room on *her* couch. She lit candles and set the table with a tablecloth, cooked spaghetti and vegan meatballs, fresh salad and chocolate truffles for me. Like a teenager trying to be an adult for the first time. The first time she had a home since I'd known her.

She gave me more coins to hold onto. I bought her a toothbrush and a phone. A few times, she put the bowler hat on, and we went for long walks in budding rose garden parks, took pictures, laughed, ate peanut butter ice cream, and talked about the future. I dreamed that she was going to make it. I knew people like her who were ten and twenty years out, still clean and thriving. I dreamed we would live together in my house with our cats and her vegan meatballs and my noddle soups. I dreamed we would ride our bikes to parties together and always have each other as dates to events. That she would come home from work and I would have dinner made and we would eat and talk about our days and read books together in bed before sleep. I dreamed about a life she never had. Maybe never wanted.

In August, her brother called. Their mom had a stroke. Or she mixed too many pills.

I said, let's go see.

Her brother was smoking when we got there. He was skinny with dark circles under his eyes and he looked just like her. He smiled.

I put a cool washcloth on her mom's forehead and held her hand. She told me how pretty I was, same as each of the handful of times I'd met her before. I smiled.

We looked into her eyes. We asked her questions like, what's your address what year is it who's the president.

She answered clearly then said, Fred is in the attic and I need to find the keys where's the oatmeal, all in one breath. We took her to the emergency room. They took her in for examination and we sat in hard plastic chairs and waited.

She said, I've been afraid my mom would die soon for a long time.

I said, I know it's really scary.

She said, I don't know what I'll do when she dies.

I wanted to say, your life will be easier when she's gone. But of course, I didn't. I hugged her and she didn't cry but I could tell she would have if the tears would've come.

The doctors said, go home she's okay we need to keep her overnight.

I said, let's go home and sleep.

I made peppermint tea and we talked in bed until we fell asleep. Her heart opened the way it does when there's a crisis. In the morning she called the hospital. Her mom had had a small stroke, but she was okay.

She took the bus to the hospital to pick up her mom and they took the bus back to her mom's apartment and stayed there. Indefinitely. Both of them. She stayed in her mom's one-bedroom apartment from then on, never going back to live with her friends, not even to get her stuff.

She said, I need to make sure she takes her medicine every day I have to get her to her follow up appointments who else is going to do it.

I said, don't stay there it's not healthy for you.

She said, it's easier this way I have to stay she wants me to stay.

I called, left messages, texted, called her mom.

When you get out of rehab they tell you not to get a job for the first year so that you won't have money to buy drugs. And so that you will have time to go to meetings. They tell you not to visit your old neighborhood so that you're not tempted. They tell you not to be in romantic relationships so you can focus on your recovery. They tell you it will be hard but keep with it, push through, go to meetings every day, we're here for you, you can do it, you can do it, you can do it. She broke all the rules.

She called once in a while and each time from a new number.

She said, it's my mom's phone my brother's phone someone gave it to me.

I said, what is going on?

She said, I just need some time, and, I'll bring back the books I borrowed tomorrow.

I said, fuck the books bring yourself back.

When the leaves started falling and it had been a few weeks, she called again.

We sat on the back steps and I said, what do you want?

And she said, you don't love me enough your walls are too high.

We don't want boundaries around our love. But there are edges to everything. We push until we feel them. And then we push some more to see how stable they are.

When the candles on the altar needed to be refreshed, my eyes re-found the coins. I picked them up one at a time. They were covered in dust and no longer felt heavy, as if they had been deflated. They felt flat and light, like when something looks heavy but when you pick it up, it's not.

About the author

Raki is a queer, Jewish fiction and poetry writer. She is the author of *The Memory House* (The Muriel Press 2019) which was a finalist for both the Red Hen Press Nonfiction Award and the Minnesota Book Award, and *The Other Body* (Dancing Girl Press 2017). Her work has appeared in numerous publications and has been nominated for several other awards, including the Pushcart Prize for fiction. She lives in Minneapolis. You can find her here: https://rakikopernik.wixsite.com/mysite and follow on Instagram @rakikopernik

Acknowledgments

Homely
Published by New Flash Fiction Review 2018

I go to parties with my cat; The red-lipped fedora girl
Published by El Balazo Press 2016

*Pressure; They Know Each Other; There's No Such Thing
As Still*
Published by Wildage Press 2015

So much gratitude for everyone who has come to my
readings, bought my books, read my stories, helped me edit,
and said nice things when I needed support. Thank you
thank you.

About the press

Unsolicited Press was established in 2012 and is based in Portland, Oregon. The team produces poetry, fiction, and nonfiction by award-winning and emerging writers.

Learn more at www.unsolicitedpress.com.

9 781950 730193